ESTHER'S CHANNEL

ESTHER'S CHANNEL

WRITTEN AND ILLUSTRATED BY

KEVIN SCOTT COLLIER

 BAKER TRITTIN PRESS

Winona Lake, Indiana

Esther's Channel
By Kevin Scott Collier

Printed in the United States of America
Cover Art: Kevin Scott Collier

Published by Baker Trittin Press
P.O. Box 277
Winona Lake, Indiana 46590

To order additional copies please call (888) 741-4386
or email info@btconcepts.com
/www.tweenertime.com or www.bakertrittinpress.com

Publishers Cataloging-Publication Data
Collier, Kevin Scott
          Esther's Channel / Kevin Scott Collier - Winona Lake,
Indiana
Baker Trittin Press, 2005

                    p.   cm.

Library of Congress Control Number: 2005925410
ISBN-10: 0-9752880-6-7
ISBN-13: 978-0-9752880-6-7
          1. Juvenile   2. Fiction   3. Religious   4. Christian
          I. Title   II. Esther's Channel

JUV033010

"The greatest act of courage is forgiveness."
‍ *Gack, the red-winged blackbird* ‍

Dedicated to
one of God's most precious
creatures in the channel of life,
Martha Claire Veldkamp.

ℰↄჿ

In loving memory of
Lois Elaine Robertson,
my "Gack" flying high watching over me,
who saw great joy in the
smallest of things.

ℰↄჿ

Character Dee Dee
dedicated to
Diane Davis.

FOREWORD

LIFE IN THE CHANNEL

For a lifetime I have regarded God's creatures as wonders that live among us. As it was as a child and still is today, I find it difficult not to pet a frog, pick up a painted turtle, or try to get as close as I can to an otter, sandpiper, or great blue heron. To me these creatures are not relegated to scenic background status but rather believed to be my kindred spirits.

So it is with great affection that I tell the tale of some of the creatures I have witnessed that live in a narrow cannel which stretches from the south end of Silver Lake (Mears, Michigan) west to the shoreline of Lake Michigan.

There is a narrow stretch of roadway that meanders through the forest beside it on which I bicycle frequently from spring to fall. Often I stop along the way to observe kindred spirits.

Cycling the path at dawn, the song of the red-winged

blackbird provides a soundtrack for a miraculous journey along the channel's banks. I have witnessed the most exquisite painted turtles resting atop logs and spied an occasional otter swimming upstream. I have held in my hands metallic blue racer snakes discovered along the channel bank. From a distance I have stood in awe of a great blue heron standing like a sentry beside a small dam. I often muse that these creatures who coexist in this peaceful channel speak with one another when I am not present and their community is not as serene as it appears but harbors fantastic secrets.

The body of water that feeds life to the channel is Silver Lake. I have often followed sandpipers along its sandy dune shoreline or caught an elusive crayfish under a dock. I have observed whimsical water bugs scamper across stagnant ponds or witnessed bullhead fish slithering along the edge of the lake's deep drop off.

But *Esther's Channel* is not really about these fascinating creatures; it's about us. It's about about people. It's about how we all affect one another. It's about the behaviors that can divide us and unite us. Most of all it's about becoming whole through forgiveness.

Rejoice in life and forever believe you have something miraculous to share with another in the channel of life. What you take for granted may be another's dream.

> Enjoy,
> *Kevin Scott Collier*

PORTRAIT GALLERY

ESTHER
the painted turtle

GACK
the red-winged blackbird

BULL BECKETT
the bullhead

BOSCO
the bullfrog

SIR ELGIN
the blue racer snake

DOODLES
the snail

MR. BERIG
the great blue heron

DEE DEE
the caterpillar

SKITTERS
the water bug

BORIS
the otter

MUMBLES
the clam

JEETER
the crayfish

MADAME SWEENEY
the elderly blanding turtle

ZIG ZAG
the sandpiper

HECTOR
the dragonfly

LORD SMYTHE
the puff ader snake

BROCK
the toad

The character Brock the toad was created by and segment dialog written by Corina Elaine Collier, 4th grade student, Thomas Read Elementary School, Shelby, Michigan.

ℰᴏ *Kevin Scott Collier* ᴄ₰

CHAPTER ONE

THE MYSTERY IN BORIS' DWELLING

A pink glow on the horizon summoned dawn as morning dew ran like tears from reeds along a quiet channel's banks. The green water moved slowly, carrying with it seeds of cottonwood like a fragile winter snow.

Narrow as a stone's throw and shallow in appearance, the channel's currents run deep with secrets.

A gentle creeping mist crawled across the warm, mirror surface as morning's first ripples announced wakening creatures.

High atop the lifeless remains of a tree, a noble red-winged blackbird surveyed the sunrise. Then he cocked his head to gaze upon the stir of life below. It was time for Gack to make a routine wake up call.

With a gracious leap, the red-winged blackbird took flight and glided down to a lodged log that rested upon the surface of the channel. A painted turtle claimed the log for her home. Gack's talons gripped the damp surface of the log as he gently came to rest upon it.

The sound of a soft snore rattled from within the beautiful painted turtle shell. Esther was sleeping inside.

"Well," Gack muttered as he hopped up onto Esther's shell. "We shall see about this."

With a shake of his feathered crown Gack arched his neck and began tapping his beak upon Esther's shell. A knocking sound, akin to a woodpecker foraging a hollow tree, began to echo in the channel.

"Esther, it is time to wake up!" a cheerful Gack announced.

"Go away!" a voice grumbled from inside the shell.

"Dear Esther, it is time to wake up," insisted the red-winged blackbird.

"Why don't you just leave me alone?" Esther shouted as her head slowly began to emerge from her shell.

"Are we in a foul mood this fine morning, Esther?" he asked.

Esther stretched her arms and legs from her shell. She blinked her yellow eyes squinting at the bright pink sparkles on the water's surface. She emitted a wide yawn and slowly turned her head to face her feathered friend,

"You seem to enjoy doing this," Esther murmured, sporting a sleepy frown.

"I shall never allow you to sleep your life away. A new day awaits you." Gack hopped back onto the log beside the turtle.

"I will never understand why you need to continue this awkward friendship of ours," Esther commented. "I can take care of myself!"

"I can take care of myself!" Gack uttered mockingly, shaking his head. "I always thought we took care of each other."

"I know the only reason you hang around is out of some twisted obligation regarding what happened when I was a baby."

"It is so pleasing when *you* tell *me* the reasons for our friendship," Gack said sarcastically. "I mean please educate me about our friendship, dear Esther."

Esther opened her eyes wide for she had been insulted and was about to respond when the impatient sound of Gack's tapping talons on her log silenced her.

"A bitter little turtle you are," he grumbled. "I am not a replacement for what you lost that day nor will I ever be. But I will always be here for you when no one else is."

Esther hung her head in shame. She slowly looked up at the red-winged blackbird as a single tear rolled down her painted cheek. "I'm sorry, Gack," Esther sobbed. "I am surprised you have stayed with me for I have been more of a disappointment to you than a friend."

"Now Esther," he spoke in a comforting tone, "that is not true."

Esther hung her head with remorse and continued to sob.

"Esther," Gack whispered, "look at me."

Esther sniffed and shook her head signaling a gentle no.

"Dear Esther," he continued, "will you *please* look at me?"

She slowly raised her head and stared into Gack's deep, black eyes.

"Do you know how special you are to me?"

Esther's lower lip quivered as she tried to regain her composure.

"You are, dear Esther, the most precious creature that lives here," he uttered softly.

Esther began to nervously scratch her log. "Do you r-r-really think so?" she stammered.

"Think? I know so!" he announced.

Esther grinned timidly as her tears subsided, "You humor me, Gack. Nothing I could ever say or do would be of any importance to you," she mumbled sadly.

Gack cackled and shook his head gently with disagreement.

"Do you know how many times I have observed you from overhead as you swim beneath the channel's surface?"

"You have watched me swim while you were in flight?" an astonished Esther replied.

"Many, many times, and always with great admiration."

"You *have* asked me often about swimming. I'm always embarrassed to describe it. It is quite boring."

"Boring to you, perhaps," Gack cackled, "but not to me."

"I thought you asked to be polite. You know . . . to show interest in things I do."

"Things I cannot do," he answered sincerely. "I cannot swim."

Esther chuckled, "Well, that is obvious. You're a bird. You fly. Flight . . . now that is a fascinating subject."

"Fascinating to you," he replied with a wide grin, "and perhaps as intriguing as the art of swimming is to me."

"But if I could only fly!" Esther said excitedly. "I have watched you so many times in flight, Gack. You have no idea how much I have dreamed of doing it."

"Then dream no more," he announced. "God gave us each other to share what makes each of us unique."

"I'm not sure I understand," Esther spoke softly to hide her confusion.

Gack hopped up onto her shell and slowly stretched out his great wings and gently moved them up and down. "Glance down at the water in the channel, Esther. Tell me what you see." He grinned with anticipation.

She looked down at the mirror surface and gasped in

amazement. "I can't believe it! Our reflection makes it appear as if I have wings."

There was more to come. Gack tightly gripped Esther's shell, bowed his head from view and began pumping his wings. Traces of blue sky and clouds above the two suddenly appeared reflecting a miraculous backdrop upon the channel's surface.

"Look, Gack, look! I'm flying!" Esther cried, "I am high above the channel, and I am touching the clouds."

Suddenly it ended. Gack stopped, folded his wings, and hopped from Esther's shell returning to his place beside her on the log.

Esther sighed with great disappointment that the illusion was over.

"It's a deception I discovered as a child," Gack explained. "If I stared at my reflection on the water long enough, I couldn't tell if my image was on the surface or below it. I imagined I could swim."

"Really?"

"It was only a deception. It didn't teach me anything about swimming."

"It didn't?" Esther was truly surprised.

"No, Esther, it was you who taught me that."

Esther blushed and responded with a wide grin.

Gack tilted his head and stared deeply into her eyes. "Never ever think of what you do as trivial, dear Esther. What you take for granted may be another's dream." He winked at the painted turtle, stretched out his wings, and with a great thrust was skyward and soon disappeared from her sight.

Esther stretched her neck and rested her head on the log. She spied Boris, the otter, swimming in her direction. His daily routine, the seemingly endless and tedious task of rebuilding his hut, had begun.

They exchanged cordial smiles as the otter passed. Boris

had a stick in his mouth as he headed upstream to his dwelling. Esther slid from her log and inquisitively began to follow the creature yet keeping her distance to avoid being noticed. She had watched his daily routine all her life. The two crossed paths repeatedly everyday, yet they had never exchanged a word. She had never been sure which mud and stick dwelling was his home.

Boris soon stopped along the channel bank. Before him was a humble dome-shaped dwelling which rose slightly above the surface of the water. Esther watched him dive underwater as he, no doubt, headed for an entrance to his home.

Esther sank below the surface and slowly paddled underwater near the dwelling. She spotted the entrance but hid behind some weeds so she would not be discovered. Soon bubbles announced Boris' exit from the passageway, and the otter darted to the surface and swam away undoubtedly in search of more sticks.

Slowly Esther parted the weeds and swam forward. She spied the entrance with apprehension and then looked around cautiously. What she was about to do, if discovered, would brand her as a trespasser by other creatures.

Territory was respected. It was one of the greatest reasons for harmony on the channel. But curiosity got the best of Esther and she swam through the entrance and came up inside Boris' hut.

When she opened her eyes, she could not believe what she saw. It was simply exquisite. The interior was a perfect half circle supported by a framework of sticks which were carefully woven then cemented into place with mud. Four evenly spaced holes in the dome provided warm light passage.

"Wow!" The sound of her own voice startled her as the interior of the dome reported an echo. "Helloo-o-o?" an amused Esther called out. She snickered at the reverb. She turned and spotted a small ledge bearing Boris' personal belongings, and she moved up to get a closer look.

There was a tiny polished black stone, a few pieces of wood gnawed into peculiar shapes, and a thin, nearly transparent scale shed from the shell of a turtle. But it wasn't a scale from just any variety of turtle. It was a scale from the shell of a *painted turtle*. She drew up closely and being curious she sniffed it. *Why would Boris have this?* she mused.

Aware of the otter's pending return, Esther realized she must leave Boris' hut. She quickly sank back into the water, exited through the hut's opening, furiously paddled a short distance, and surfaced. When she focused her eyes on the water ahead, an alarmed Esther saw Boris heading straight toward her.

She kept her composure, and the two exchanged cordial smiles as they passed each other. "Whew," Esther whispered, "that was close."

A sudden movement to her left caught her attention, and she turned her head. It was Sir Elgin, the blue racer snake, slithering across the surface of the channel in Esther's direction.

The painted turtle quickly faced straight ahead and paddled onward to ignore the creature.

"Acch" sounded Sir Elgin as if to clear his throat. "Excuse me?"

Esther acted as though she didn't hear him.

"May I have a word with you, Esther?" Sir Elgin called out loudly.

A sick feeling brushed over the turtle. "I'm busted," she mumbled under her breath. She ceased paddling and slowed almost to a halt as Sir Elgin glided to her side.

"I couldn't help but notice," he exclaimed with an imposing stare, "how alarmingly close you were to Boris' hut when you surfaced but a moment ago."

Esther swallowed hard and tried to avoid eye contact. Sir Elgin grinned as he observed the turtle's suspicious behavior.

"You wouldn't have, by chance," the snake inquired, "been snooping around the otter's dwelling, would you?"

"Not re-e-eally," Esther stuttered.

"Really, Esther? I've come to accept your mischievious ways, but lying is never acceptable." Sir Elgin shook his head with disappointment.

"Well, so what if I did snoop a little?" Esther glowered. "It's not like you can tell my mother about it."

Sir Elgin hissed and replied, "*That* was uncalled for, Esther."

She drew back into her shell and blinked.

"I have long abandoned seeking your forgiveness about that day," he said, "but I've never given up hope for you, Esther."

She slowly poked her head from her shell and her eyes met the blue racer's. "I'm sorry," she said, "but what did you see?"

"I only saw you surface near the hut, nothing else. But I believe your conscience has just revealed the rest," Sir Elgin replied with a grin.

"You won't tell Gack, will you?" Esther asked anxiously.

"No, but how would you feel if you were to discover Boris was stripping away wood from your log while you were away?"

"I would be mad!" she snarled.

"Boris would never do such a thing," Sir Elgin assured. "Even though you two have never become friends, he respects you and your property."

Esther pondered the thought as the two floated slowly in the gentle current of the channel. But one greater thing was on Esther's mind. It was the mystery inside the otter's dwelling, and she could keep the secret no longer.

"Um."

"Yes?" Sir Elgin was quick to respond.

"I found a painted turtle shell scale in Boris' hut. Why would Boris keep such a thing and for what reason?"

"I have no clue."

"I wonder who would know?" Esther muttered.

"You could ask Gack," Sir Elgin suggested with a grin, "but of course, you would have to reveal how you would know such a thing exists inside the otter's dwelling."

"In other words confess my sin?"

"Confession is good for the soul," the snake replied. "Gack does seem to know many secrets of the channel."

Esther thought for a moment, "Perhaps I can tell Gack that Boris told me about the turtle shell scale."

"Simply unbelieveable," Sir Elgin laughed. "Everyone in the channel knows you and Boris have never exchanged a single word."

"But maybe today we did speak and Boris told me of it."

"Unlikely," he chuckled. "Secrets are shared with only the closest friends. If Boris had told you about it, he likely would have explained its significance too. Simply tell Gack the truth."

"I shall have to give this some thought," Esther mumbled feeling quite distressed.

"Then I shall leave you. Leave you to let your conscience do battle with your curiosity." With that parting comment and an accusing grin, Sir Elgin slithered across the channel onto the shoreline. Esther watched as the blue racer snake vanished into the brush.

Suddenly Esther sensed someone was following her, so she snaked her head backward to take a look. She spied Bosco, the bullfrog, darting across the surface of the water in suspicious pursuit.

"Oh brother," Esther mumbled and turned her head and faced

forward.

"Well, if it isn't naughty little Esther," the bullfrog sneered.

Ignoring the frog, Esther continued to paddle forward.

"It is simply amazing how well the sound carries in the channel on calm mornings like this." Bosco was now swimming beside her as he continued, "Oh my, my, my the pieces of conversations you hear."

Esther scowled and continued to ignore the creature.

"As an example," and the bullfrog paused just long enough, "the bit of chatter I heard just moments ago between you and Sir Elgin about the otter and the secret."

Anxious and panic stricken, Esther swallowed deeply and addressed the frog. "W-w-what did you hear?" she stuttered.

"Well, you tell me." Bosco snickered with an evil grin on his face.

"You heard nothing."

"Maybe I, too, should leave you to let your conscience do battle with your curiosity," the bullfrog chuckled slyly.

Esther gulped and stammered, "I d-d-don't know what you are talking about."

"Perhaps I shall just have to tell Gack all about it," Bosco sneered triumphantly and began to swim away.

"W-w-wait!' Esther called.

"You're up to no good. I know it. You never listened to rules as a child, and you have no respect for them today." Bosco glowered at the frightened turtle.

"Maybe we can keep this between Sir Elgin, you, and I?" Esther pleaded. "There is no need to run to Gack with this. I don't need to know what the mystery is behind the scale."

"The scale?" Bosco mumbled curiously.

"You know. . . ." She stopped suddenly and looked at Bosco

with suspicion.

An awkward Bosco tried to regain his composure.

"Well, well," he said, "yes, of course, the mysterious scale."

Esther frowned. She no longer believed the creature.

"I can only guess the fish must have been huge," she answered with a grin.

"Yes, a monster of a fish no doubt," Bosco replied cautiously while trying to read Esther's expression. "But I heard Sir Elgin appeal to you to tell Gack the truth about it."

"Yes," Esther said, raising her chin, "and it will take courage to do so."

"And Boris is somehow involved I hear."

"I'm not too sure of that. We've never spoken you know."

"Then how would Boris know anything about the monster fish?" Bosco was confused.

"That's the mystery," Esther replied with a smug look on her face.

Bosco shook his green and yellow head with suspicion. "You sound as if you are making all this up," the bullfrog said with a rattle of anger in his voice.

"How can I be?" Esther shot back. "You, yourself, have heard of it. Are you making it up?"

"Enough of this foolish nonsense," Bosco grunted.

Esther looked ahead, keeping her face without expression.

"I warn you, Esther, if I find you have done something wrong," Bosco sneered, "I shall tell Gack."

With that the angry bullfrog swam off to his lily pad.

CHAPTER TWO

ESTHER'S SECRET FRIEND

Esther's curiosity concerning the mysterious turtle shell scale faded as she paddled by a familiar stretch of milkweed plants along the channel's bank. Esther snuck toward the shore to pay Dee Dee, the timid caterpillar, a visit.

The caterpillar and the turtle shared a special bond no one else in the channel knew of. Dee Dee was Esther's secret friend. As she rummaged through the milkweed plants ashore, something was amiss.

The caterpillar was always the first to offer greetings but not this time.

"Dee Dee," Esther called out.

There was no answer. *Where could she be,* Esther thought to herself as her observant eyes darted about the area. She pushed on with great concern.

"Dee Dee, where are you?" She stopped suddenly as something strange caught her eye.

"What is that?" Esther asked softly as she crawled up to an odd shaped object hanging from a milkweed plant. She examined it closely, sniffing at the object's smooth golden surface. Then she gasped in horror.

"Dee Dee!" Esther cried. The identification was unmistakable. Whatever this silky woven object was, the caterpillar was trapped hopelessly inside of it.

"Dee Dee!" a panicked Esther screamed at her tiny friend.

But there was no response. There was no motion. Esther began to back up shuddering with fright.

"Who would do such a thing?" she sobbed. Her tearful eyes were fixed on the silky shroud. "Who would kill my secret friend?"

The devastated Esther wept as she scrambled through the milkweeds retreating quickly to the safety of the channel.

Ravaged with grief she dove beneath the surface of the channel and headed to the bottom. She navigated wildly through a maze of broken submerged trees. Frantically she maneuvered a web of algae-covered branches twisting and turning as she passed through. Exhausted and out of breath she surfaced at the shore and gasped for air as she crawled up onto the bank.

She drew her eyes into focus. She was startled at what was in front of her, two large slender feet with sharp taloned toes. Slowly Esther tilted her head upward and followed a long set of bony legs to a massive feathered torso. At the very top of the creature a head arched slightly downward as the huge bird spied the turtle.

It was Mr. Berig, the great blue heron.

Mr. Berig's eyes opened wide with surprise. Uneasiness swept over the great bird as he took two steps backward and nervously cleared his throat.

"H-h-hello, Esther," Mr. Berig spoke awkwardly.

The last time Esther had been this close to Mr. Berig was when she was a baby. That was a memory best forgotten.

Esther snorted as her blood began to boil. Her eyes squinted and she emitted an angry hiss.

A rejected Mr. Berig took two more steps backward.

"You ruined my life, you monster!" a fearless Esther shouted at the enormous bird. "I shall *never* forgive you for that."

Mr. Berig briefly dropped his head in shame and then raised it in a weak display of dignity.

"I am truly sorry," the great blue heron muttered with remorse.

She glared at the great blue heron with anger as she slowly backed into the waters of the channel and disappeared below the surface.

She darted with sheer panic through the submerged branches as if they were fingers from her past returning to grip her. She began to slow and grow calm.

She surfaced to see her log up ahead and paddled to it with a sense of security. Esther crawled atop it sniffing the bark and scratching it as if to mark her territory. She drew her neck out as far as it would go and rested her head upon the wood.

Suddenly a flurry of feathers sounded above announcing Gack's arrival. The red-winged blackbird touched down beside Esther on her log.

"A lovely day," Gack said with a grin. "Would you not agree?"

"I have something to tell you and something to ask you," Esther whispered in an embarrassed manner.

"All right," an attentive Gack said.

"What I did was wrong," she admitted, "and I don't need a lecture. I am sorry I did it, and I'll never do it again."

Gack started impatiently tapping his talons on Esther's log.

"Well then, what is it?"

"Promise you will not yell at me?"

"Well . . . ok."

"I went inside Boris' dwelling uninvited."

"You *whaaat*?" Gack shouted.

"You promised!" Esther reminded him.

"All right!" replied a disappointed Gack. "But trespassing another's dwelling. My word, dear Esther."

She hung her head in shame.

"You have a question?" he asked as he quickly regained his composure.

"Boris has a small ledge inside of his hut," she explained. "On it is a scale shed from the shell of a painted turtle. Why would Boris keep something like that? Where did it come from?"

Gack's eyes opened wide with surprise, and he struggled to find the right words. "It is a memory Boris keeps," he said nervously.

"Yes, but a memory of whom?"

"I *cannot* reveal this to you."

Esther twisted her face, expressing first her confusion then her surprise. "You know, but you won't say?"

"It is private," Gack whispered. "I know who the scale is from and why it is there."

"Some friend you are," Esther grumbled.

"I shall speak no more of this!" he answered sternly.

"Well, um, err. . . ." Esther stammered. "Well, who can I talk with to find out more about it?"

"You could talk with Boris. But if you brought up the scale, you would make him aware that you had trespassed his dwelling."

"I d-d-don't want to do that," Esther sputtered.

"Then this shall remain a mystery to you."

Esther sighed with disappointment.

"Why be so glum, dear Esther?" Gack asked. "Perhaps one day . . . if you have the courage to discover who Boris really is, you will have the astonishing answer to that mystery." With that Gack smugly grinned, leaped into the sky, and flew over the treetops.

Esther lowered her head slowly on to the log and enjoyed the warm sunshine. She began to think about her past and the day she first encountered Gack. A chill struck her, and she did not wish to remember the circumstances surrounding their bond.

She began to recall events moments before meeting Gack and a creature she met below the surface of the water that day. It was a tiny creature that first gave her hope that all of her dreams would come true.

Esther's eyes grew anxious but heavy and quickly she fell into a deep sleep. Her mind's eye went to black as she traveled backward in time. She heard the gentle sound of the flowing channel water, and from the darkness emerged a bright light.

A mostly submerged, capsized wreckage of a wooden rowboat came into view. The bow, which rose just above the waterline, revealed the vessel's original yellow painted surface. The remainder, beneath the surface, was covered green from weeds and algae.

It was Esther's forbidden childhood playground. Baby Esther paddled to it and cautiously surveyed her surroundings. She spotted Sir Elgin, the blue racer snake, on the channel's bank. Their eyes met, and the snake struck a look of horror in his eyes.

"Uh-oh I'm busted," Esther mumbled to herself as she dove beneath the surface of the water to avoid being seen. She headed to the submerged rowboat.

Sir Elgin quickly slithered into the channel and raced upstream.

Safely below the surface, Esther journeyed inside the boat.

There she joyfully paddled between the algae-covered plank seats and the floorboards as if she were exploring a great shipwreck.

She playfully nudged a small piece of tattered weed-laced rope tied to an oarlock. Frightened minnows scattered as she observed the stern of the boat which was partially buried in the murky channel bottom.

Esther noticed a thin meandering line on the hull of the boat. It was a narrow path so clean it revealed the yellow paint beneath the algae-covered wood. It was as if something had carefully etched the line. She sniffed the scribbles inquisitively and began to follow where they led.

Suddenly her nose bumped into something small and hard. "Ouch!" she cried.

"Hey!" a tiny voice followed. It was a very disturbed little snail.

"Oops! Excuse me," Esther said apologetically.

"My word," the snail shouted disgustedly.

"I said I was sorry," she retorted as she closely observed the creature.

"You really should watch where you are going!"

"Oh my goodness!" Esther cried with excitement. "Y-y-you have a shell."

"Why yes, I do."

"Well, so do I."

"You are quite small for a painted turtle," the snail observed. "You must be a baby."

Esther nodded a timid yes.

"Sorry I grumbled at you."

"Your apology is accepted. You're very small. Are you a baby too?"

"Mmmphhh!" choked the snail. "I am most certainly not a

30

baby. I am an adult, and it would please me if you would remove your snout from my face."

Esther quickly drew her head back and grinned. "What's your name?"

"Doodles. And how shall I address you?"

Esther was confused.

"What is your name, child? I trust you have a name."

"Oh yes, I have a name. It's Esther."

"A sweet name," Doodles responded pleasantly. "Such a sweet name for such an exquisite little turtle."

Esther blushed and struck a wide smile.

"I do have to ask," his voice changed to a more serious tone, "should you be playing here?"

She assumed a suspicious posture, "Why s-s-sure. I p-p-play here a lot," Esther answered nervously.

The crusty snail shook his antennae-topped head with uncertainty. "This is usually the cut-off point down channel for children," he explained. "I'm sure you know why."

"Of c-c-course," Esther stammered, "b-b-but I have permission to play here."

Doodles eyed her doubtfully. "Telling fibs can have serious results sometimes, Esther."

His comment unsettled her, but she managed an exaggerated smile.

"Well, just stay close to the boat," he pleaded.

A timid yes was all she managed. Once again she quickly began inquisitively observing the thin trail the snail had left on the surface of the sunken boat. "Why do you leave drawings wherever you go? They are quite beautiful."

"Pardon me?" the clueless snail answered.

"Those squiggly lines you leave behind you."

"Oh those," Doodles chuckled. "As I move, I leave a path of where I've been."

"So the path will guide you back home?"

"No!" the snail snickered. "No reason at all. It is simply a result of my crawling."

Esther continued looking at the twisting lines. "Have you ever followed your own path backward, Doodles?"

"Why would anyone wish to go backward?" he asked in a surprised tone. "It would be like returning to your past. Who would ever wish to do that?"

"You never look back?"

"No, and neither should you, Esther. Where you are headed is more important than where you have been."

Esther looked confused, and Doodles just rolled his beady eyes.

"Esther, what do you hope for in life when you grow up?"

"Oh, I can imagine many things."

"Such as?"

"I will always live in the channel. I will have my own log. I will have lots of friends." Her enthusiasm was evident. "And no matter how grown up I become, I will always wish to be close to my mother."

"You plan to stay here by her side?"

"Oh yes. She is everything to me," Esther whispered.

"Your love for your mother must be truly great. Most creatures want to move on," Doodles observed.

"Move on? Not me," Esther stubbornly insisted. "I'm staying right here by my mom!"

Doodles chuckled and muttered, "I'm sure your mother will be very proud of you some day, Esther. I know she will always adore you."

Esther suddenly remembered Sir Elgin had spotted her near

the boat. She began looking around nervously. "I really should be on my way."

"If I should never see you again, Esther, I do hope all your dreams come true," Doodles announced.

Esther darted away from the wreckage of the rowboat and headed to the water's surface.

When she came up, she noticed she was slightly down the channel from the bow of the boat. She began to swim upstream toward it, but no matter how hard she tried it appeared she was not moving.

Suddenly Esther felt something on her nose.

As she twitched her snout, all before her became dark. Her dream was ending, and she was returning to the present. As she opened her eyes, they went crossed as she tried to focus on the beautiful blue and green dragonfly standing on the tip of her nose.

She was dreaming no more.

Esther had an unexpected visitor.

"Oh, I am very sorry," the surprised dragonfly said. "I assumed you were a part of this log."

Esther grumbled as the bug jumped from her nose and gently landed in front of her upon the log's dry bark surface.

"You look confused," the dragonfly said, "and sleepy."

"I am," she muttered. "Both."

"What's your name?"

"I am Esther," the painted turtle replied with a yawn. "You would be?"

"Hector," he announced. "Hey, do you live here?"

"Yes, all of my life."

"I live out in Silver Lake," he announced proudly. "It's a much more exciting place than this I assure you."

"I've heard it's dangerous."

"Nonsense! You have lived in this channel all your life. How lame is that?

"It's pretty boring, Hector," Esther admitted. She surveyed her familiar surroundings before adding, "It's safe though. Better safe than sorry."

"Silver Lake is just up the channel," he explained and motioned a wing in its direction. Have you ever imagined what it is like outside of this narrow existence?"

"I have thought of it."

"You don't appear to be very happy. It probably has to do with this channel."

"There are issues here between me and some of my neighbors," she muttered.

"I can't believe you have lived in this narrow water pathway all of your life," Hector mumbled, shaking his tiny head.

"It's true," Esther sighed. "I have never gone anywhere else."

"Pathways are meant to lead somewhere," the insect said. "Upstream is your destiny!"

Esther's eyes grew very bright as she glanced upstream, and she took a deep breath. "I've often wondered what it would be like elsewhere."

"Then you should think about what you want to do with the rest of your life," he challenged. "Do you know what you really need to do? You need to go find yourself. You need to get off this pathetic rotting log and expand your horizons. Silver Lake is a nice place to start."

Esther stared at the old log beneath her and mumbled, "Find myself?"

"Yeah," the dragonfly replied. "Get in touch with who you are. Best of all, when you journey to other places, you leave what troubles you behind."

34

"Really?"

"Oh yeah, big time," Hector gushed with pride. "Look at me. I'm free to journey as I please. I'm making new friends all the time. It's a sweet existence."

"It's not sweet here, and the issues in the channel will *never* be resolved."

"You need some adventure in your life, kid! Start with a tour of the lake." He sounded like a salesman. "If that's not your thing, move on elsewhere. The only one stopping you is you."

Esther looked all around and sighed. "P-p-perhaps I could at least see what lies beyond this channel." There was reluctance in her voice. "If I don't feel comfortable, I can always return."

"Now that's a start," Hector encouraged her with a striking grin. "Give it a shot. You will never know until you try."

"Perhaps I should at least say goodbye to Gack."

"What's a Gack?" giggled Hector.

"He's a red-winged blackbird," Esther said a little defensively, "and he's my friend."

"Obviously he's free to travel anywhere he pleases in a moment's notice," Hector snickered. "Why not just split this stagnant ditch now?"

"Yeah, he's free to go anywhere he wishes," Esther grumbled. "Why shouldn't I?"

"Now you're talking, kid!" Hector chuckled. With that final comment Hector flew off leaving Esther to ponder her plight and her future.

She scratched at the parched bark on her log and muttered, "Find myself. . ."

Slowly the painted turtle crawled to the edge and slipped off into the channel.

Esther began to paddle upstream beyond Bosco's lily pads,

past Boris' dwelling, and under Termite Bridge. She was anxious as she journeyed farther than she had ever been upstream.

Uncertainty washed over her.

Ahead in the distance a large lake was beginning to appear. And with it came the hope of finding herself.

CHAPTER THREE

BULL BECKETT AND MADAME SWEENEY

As Esther paddled out into Silver Lake, her eyes widened. She had never seen such a great body of water. She had never felt so small, and she had never viewed such great promise.

On the distant horizon there were cottages along the shore. To her left and ahead was a large sand dune that bordered one side of the lake, and the sun reflected brightly off of it. An inviting cove was nearby, rich with lily pads and cattails.

Esther dipped her face below the water's surface and saw logs and weeds beneath her. Unlike the channel, the lake was deep.

It beckoned her.

She dove beneath the surface and began to slip into the darkness. She had never felt so free.

Suddenly the serenity of the moment was broken by the sound of vicious thrashing nearby. Drawn to the fury, Esther cautiously swam in its direction. A murky dark image quickly came into view. A large bullhead with a hook in its mouth was violently tugging a line which reached to the water's surface.

Esther's yellow eyes opened wide with fear. She knew what she was witnessing. She could see the bottom of a boat floating on the lake's surface.

Fishermen lurked above.

Near defeat, the thrashing stopped briefly as the bullhead made one final desperate dive. Mercifully the line snapped, freeing the creature.

Exhausted, the fish slowly descended motionless, coming to rest upon the muddy lake bottom. Esther followed.

"Are you all right?" she asked with concern.

"What do you want?" the creature grumbled, working its bleeding jaw.

"The hook is still in your mouth! Perhaps I can remove it for you."

"And for this I will owe you what?"

"Nothing."

"What is your name, turtle?" the bullhead snarled.

"E-E-Esther. I come from the channel. W-W-Who are you?"

The bullhead's hollow black eyes narrowed with suspicion.

"My name is Bull Beckett. You can attempt to remove the hook, but do not expect any favor for doing so."

A frightened Esther drew closer, carefully observing the hook and line.

"I-I-I think I can do it, but this may hurt."

"Pain is the least of my worries, turtle," growled the bullhead.

"Here we go." She squinted as her beak clamped down on the hook. With one swift move the hook dislodged and came gently to rest on the lake bottom.

"Don't expect a thank you," said a wincing Bull Beckett.

An astonished Esther blinked.

"But, I only wanted to. . . ." Esther began.

"Be on your way, turtle," he snarled. "Your kind sickens me."

A shunned Esther raised her head in defiance and bravely followed the creature as he slowly slithered away.

"What *is* your problem?"

"Get lost," Bull Beckett grumbled.

"Are you so bitter that you cannot even answer me?"

The bullhead came to an abrupt stop and turned his menacing head in Esther's direction.

"I don't answer to anyone! Especially not to land dwellers such as yourself."

"I am a creature of water, too!" Esther snapped back.

"Only when you choose. Pathetic, lazy, no good freaks . . . that's your kind."

In anger Esther rammed Bull Beckett with her head, knocking the creature off balance.

"So it's a fight you want, *is it?*" Bull Beckett scoffed as he drew his sharp-pronged stinger fins in Esther's direction.

"You meddlesome pest!" the bullhead glowered as he bolted in attack.

Esther quickly turned her body to fend off the attack. Bull Beckett's venomous spikes harmlessly grazed Esther's shell as he rapidly swept past her. The impact of the turbulence sent Esther reeling.

The bullhead turned sharply coming round for a second attack as Esther thrust her arms and legs out furiously to regain her balance.

Suddenly a sharp powerful slice broke through the water. Instantly both were alarmed.

SWOOOOOOSH!

"*Spears!*" Bull Beckett cried out as a second sharp-pronged rod with line in tow shot past Esther's head, plowing into the mucky lake bottom.

"They don't care who they kill!" the bullhead barked in anger.

Esther drew her head upward and her eyes caught a shifting reflection above the surface. Another spear was being drawn back.

"Get out of the way!" Esther cried, ramming the bullhead clear of the bolting metal rod.

"That was too close," Bull Beckett shuddered as the two rapidly fled the danger zone.

Things were very quiet for the next few moments. The two slowly surveyed their surroundings.

"It looks safe here," the bullhead assured.

A wide-eyed Esther simply nodded in agreement and swallowed hard.

"Not like the comfy life in the channel, is it?" Bull Beckett snickered.

"N-n-not at all." Esther replied, noticing for the first time large scars etching the bottom-feeder's smooth, black skin. Apparently the bullhead had encountered these spear fishermen before.

Bull Beckett cocked his head and sported a bloody grin.

"Creatures grow up hard out here, Esther. Survival doesn't allow for kindness. Today's friend may be tomorrow's predator."

"Y-Y-Yes sir," Esther stammered.

"I don't hate you, kid," the bullhead murmured, glancing at Esther, "but to make it in this world you can never trust anyone but yourself."

Esther shook her head with disbelief.

"Do you know what happens, Esther, when you make a friend out here?"

"No."

"You end up dead!" the bullhead growled. "Want to be dead, Esther?"

A chilling silence brushed over the turtle.

As the bullhead and the turtle parted ways, Esther didn't even say goodbye to the tormented fish. A silent mutual nod would have to do.

Esther surfaced and checked her surroundings and saw that the fishing boat was headed off in the distance. She spotted a shallow cove nearby, and the beauty of it drew her in.

As Esther headed toward the swampy cove, she stretched her neck above the water's surface and felt the warm sunshine upon her face. Hope was returning.

Surveying the new surroundings, she spotted a log much like her home in the channel and swam to it.

As soon as she had climbed on, she heard a fury flutter above her and looked up. It was Gack, the red-winged blackbird, preparing to land on her log.

"Enjoying your little vacation, Esther?" Gack said smugly, touching down next to her on the log.

"What are you doing? Checking up on me again?" Esther spoke her disapproval.

"Oh, dear Esther, how you let that imagination of yours run wild," Gack cackled.

"I've left the channel to find a new life, and I've already met one new friend," Esther said, turning her nose up to snub the bird.

"A new life?"

"Yes, *and* a new friend," Esther sneered.

"Oh really? Please do tell me, dear Esther, who this marvelous creature may be."

Gack began tapping his talons impatiently on the sun-parched log.

"It's none of your business!" Esther snapped.

"The best thing about being a bird, Esther, is the vantage points." Esther slowly turned her head in his direction and gave him one of her best frowns.

"I may not swim, but from above I can, at times, see what goes on below the surface of the water."

Esther remained silent.

"That gruesome fish you were traveling with wouldn't by chance have been Bull Beckett, would it?"

Esther said nothing.

"I think your silence just answered that," Gack replied as Esther's frown crunched a bit more.

"You don't need to go below the surface of the water to hear about the likes of a character such as Bull Beckett. I have heard much about him, none of it admirable, of course," Gack reported in a scolding tone. "Is this your new friend, Esther? I sincerely doubt it."

"You think you know everything," Esther mumbled.

"I know enough about a creature like Bull Beckett that he would never be your friend," Gack replied.

"He's just tormented and very opinionated, that's all."

"Aren't we all? But a friend he's not!" Gack snapped. "He doesn't like land dwellers, and he doesn't approve of friendships. He probably told you to get lost. Would that be correct?"

After a deep sigh, Esther muttered, "Yes."

"Hey, it's not your fault."

"Is Bull Beckett a creature without a soul?" Esther asked.

"Well, he certainly lacks a conscience," Gack replied.

"What's a conscience?" Esther inquired.

"It is the little voice inside that directs us on a righteous path in life. Without it we would never feel guilt, or shame, or remorse."

"It sounds rather chilling."

"The most chilling thing of all, Esther, is that these creatures without a conscience are unaware of the havoc they wreak upon others without regard," he explained. "It's either that, or they simply don't care."

Gack sidled up next to Esther, patted his feathers reassuringly upon her shell and tilted his head to her face.

"Not all creatures out here are the likes of Bull Beckett," he whispered softly. "Do not let disappointment defeat your journey."

"H-h-he basically said you can only trust yourself, and if you have f-f-friends, you end up dead," Esther stuttered.

Gack tilted his head closer and tapped his beak on the tip of Esther's nose. "Chin up, child," he whispered. "It's one bad experience, that's all."

Esther straightened her head and peered into Gack's shiny black eyes.

"My goodness! 'Make friends and you end up dead'!" Gack crowed, shaking his feathered crown. "What a thing to say."

"Bull Beckett said the only one you can trust is yourself," Esther mumbled beneath her breath.

"Rubbish, Esther, Bull Beckett is wrong," Gack glowered. "Friends give you a reason to live, and friendships are built on trust."

Esther blinked slowly as if ashamed.

"Do you recall the day we became friends, dear Esther?"

"Y-y-yes," Esther stuttered.

"It was the day I saved your life," Gack said proudly.

Esther nodded in recognition.

"That, dear Esther, is an example of how friendships work. Friendships provide safety and strength in numbers," Gack explained. "Who you really should talk to out here is Madame Sweeney."

"Madame Sweeney?" Esther replied curiously. "Who is that?"

"This is your journey; you find out. She's on the other side of this cove under that willow tree," he replied, pointing his beak in the direction.

Esther spied the area and nodded with approval.

"Best be nice to her." Gack commanded, winking an eye as he lifted off into flight.

Esther rolled her eyes as she slid from the log and swam back into the cove. She began paddling in the direction of the willow tree.

Suddenly a winged shadow traveled over Esther on the surface of the water. She looked upward with alarm. It was Mr. Berig, the great blue heron, in flight. He touched down on the shore not far from the willow tree. Esther watched the creature as it plucked a small fish from the water to eat.

Esther reached the willow tree and pulled herself up onto a damp web of roots that stretched out into the water.

Her heart raced with anger at the sight of the great blue heron in the distance. She was startled by a shaky voice that pierced the moment.

"You need not fear that creature," the strange voice spoke.

"W-w-what?" Esther said, cocking her head in the direction of the voice.

"Mr. Berig is harmless, unless of course, you are a small

fish," added the stranger.

Sitting in a nook of willow tree roots was an elderly female blanding turtle. Esther's yellow eyes became wide with curiosity. She had never seen a turtle such as this in the channel.

"Pardon me, but you are so strikingly beautiful," Esther said in awe.

"If I am beautiful, it is because of who I am and not for my appearance," the elderly turtle replied with a grin.

Esther did not reply but just stared with awesome curiosity.

"You are not from here," the elderly turtle observed, stretching out her yellow neck. "Are you lost?"

Esther snapped out of her gaze.

"Um, I am trying to find myself, Ma'am," Esther replied.

"Well, if you seek to find yourself, I declare that I have just found you," the blanding turtle laughed. "You are lost no more!"

Esther grinned, then added, "I am looking for Madame Sweeney."

"Then I have been found also," Madame Sweeney nodded. "It appears now we have found each other."

Esther broke into a brief smile before striking a serious tone.

"Gack sent me," she announced.

"Gack? How would you know him and who might you be?" Madame Sweeney attentively focused her ancient eyes on Esther.

"I am Esther from the channel, and Gack is my friend."

"Say no more. I know exactly who you are," the blanding turtle replied, "Gack has spoken of you. You, Miss Esther, harbor resentment. *Tsk, tsk.*"

Esther sat motionless, reluctant to respond.

"You blame others," Madame Sweeney spoke softly, shaking her head with disapproval.

Esther was uncomfortable with Gack's disclosure to this wise old turtle, and she began to shift her body anxiously.

"You don't understand," she said cautiously.

"Wisdom comes with time, and I have lived forever," said Madame Sweeney with a rattle in her voice. "I have outlived all of my children and countless friends, too."

Esther stared into Madame Sweeney's dark eyes as if they were deep pits. A warm sparkle glowed within them.

"Understanding is one of my finest qualities, Esther." Madame Sweeney tilted her head upward before continuing. "I also know a great deal about loss."

"Y-y-yes, Ma'am," Esther stammered.

It seemed like a lifetime of silence, but it was only seconds before the blanding turtle said something that made Esther gasp.

"I knew your mother, Esther."

Esther's mouth went agape.

"When she discovered she was carrying you, she made her way to the channel to find a safer home. She had witnessed my grief losing children out here in the lake and would have none of it," Madame Sweeney explained. "How ironic that now I speak with the offspring of the friend I lost."

"I'm sorry," Esther muttered.

"Sorry? For what, child?" Madame Sweeney replied, breaking into a slight grin.

"It was my fault," Esther mumbled.

"So now it's your fault? I thought Gack told me you blamed others," snorted Madame Sweeney.

"I would rather not talk about this," Esther appealed, hanging her head.

"Don't you have many friends, dear?" the Blanding turtle asked. "Friendships are blessings, Esther."

"Bull Beckett said we are better off without friends." That

provoked laughter from Madame Sweeney.

"Bull Beckett? Bull Beckett? My word! You choose to listen to that selfish creature?" Madame Sweeney asked. "To be selfish, Esther, is to always be alone."

"He said the only one you can trust is yourself," Esther solemnly added.

"I once told Bull Beckett when he was a youth that he will never feel his heart until he considers others," Madame Sweeney snapped.

"He did seem rather heartless."

"Oh, Bull Beckett has a heart, dear Esther. We all do. He just needs to find it."

"I see," Esther answered as she crawled up next to Madame Sweeney and released a huge sigh.

"The day Bull Beckett shows compassion for another he will be whole," the wise old turtle remarked.

Esther looked ahead of her and watched the bright ripples on the surface of the cove. She began to feel a void.

"How do you live with . . . loss, Madame Sweeney?" Esther inquired with hesitation.

"You mean how do you overcome loss?" The blanding turtle sought to clarify the question.

"Yes," Esther nodded.

"It's done by living a life with purpose and keeping their memory alive. It is our obligation to those we lose," Madame Sweeney whispered. Then she added in a terse tone, "Gack says you never speak of your mother. Shame on you."

Esther snaked her head inside of her shell and trembled.

Madame Sweeney took a deep breath, regained her composure, and her voice softened.

"You really should talk to others about your mother, Esther,"

Madame Sweeney said warmly.

"I know," Esther whimpered.

"The essence of all she was is within you. You have an obligation to her memory."

Esther began to shed a silent tear.

"She did not leave you, dear," Madame Sweeney said as she looked into Esther's shell. "She's within you, Esther. Can't you feel her? She talks to you every day. Do you ever listen to her?"

Madame Sweeney pulled back as Esther slowly poked her head out from her shell and focused on Madame Sweeney's dark, wise eyes.

"Perhaps instead of attempting to find yourself, you should look inside and rediscover her. Once you do, I promise you, Esther, you will find yourself."

Esther looked at Madame Sweeney and blinked away a tear.

"I will try to do that," promised Esther.

"Then be on your journey." Lowering her voice she added, "Esther, you cannot run away from what troubles you. Despair is like the shell which covers you. No matter where you journey it will always be with you."

Esther gestured a shrug of uncertainty.

"I believe what weighs heavy on your heart must be resolved back in the channel. Until it is, it will be a burden you will carry, sweet Esther," advised Madame Sweeney.

"Thank you for your time," said a hurried Esther. "I must be on my way."

Madame Sweeney stretched out her wrinkled golden neck and kissed Esther on the cheek.

"My prayers are with you, sweet child."

Esther put her chin up as she crawled from the willow tree's roots and back into the inviting calm water.

Madame Sweeney sighed as she watched Esther paddle across the cove and out of the sight.

CHAPTER FOUR

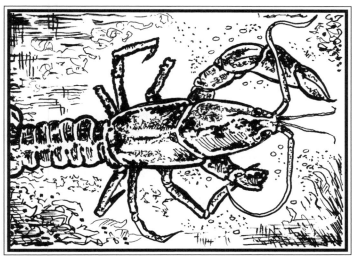

JEETER AND MUMBLES

Esther brushed the rich green lily pads as she navigated through the cove and smelled their fragrant white and yellow flowers. She whimsically zigzagged through velvety cattails like an obstacle course. She stopped for a moment and hope filled her heart once again.

As she reached the shore on the other side of the cove, a strange ripple movement in the shallow water attracted her attention. She slowly paddled toward it unsure of what she was confronting. A voice broke her concentration.

"What are you going to do? Eat me?" a tiny gravelly voice questioned.

Esther searched carefully and saw something poking its head above the surface of the water.

"Pardon me?" was Esther's guarded reply. Soon she clearly

saw the crayfish.

"I said, shell head, are you going to eat me?" the crayfish grumbled.

"Certainly not!"

The crayfish twitched its feelers and focused its beady little black eyes upon Esther.

"I have never seen you before," he observed.

"I recognize your kind. There are crabs just like you in the channel," Esther replied.

"The channel? Oh, the good life, huh?" the crayfish snickered and began to crawl with a limp up the mucky cove bank. Esther followed.

"My name is Esther. Who are you?"

"My name is Jeeter, and I am not a crab," the crayfish answered, obviously suspicious.

Once on land, Esther noticed Jeeter was missing one of his claw-tipped arms and two of his legs. Esther's mouth went agape as she stared in horror.

"Didn't anyone ever tell you that it's rude to stare at another's misfortune?" glowered Jeeter.

"I'm v-v-very sorry," Esther stammered, embarrassed and concerned that she had offended the creature.

"I got into a rather nasty altercation," the crayfish explained as he held up what was once an arm with pincer. He looked at the useless stump.

"Tragic!" Esther shuddered.

"It was either lose a few limbs and escape the situation or die. Living is always better. You can cope with the rest," he added philosophically.

Esther nodded and gave Jeeter an awkward but friendly smile.

"Sorry to be so crabby, kid," he mumbled with a grin.

"Sorry I stared," Esther replied in a rather somber tone.

"Don't worry about it. I've been through this before, and I have learned to live with it."

"How unfortunate." Esther's voice indicated her concern.

Jeeter uttered an unsettled chuckle.

"Esther, I am luckier than most. My limbs will grow back!" he explained. "Others are not so fortunate. If you lost a leg, you would never see it return, so I count my blessings."

"Oh, I see," she stated, not sure what else to say.

"I have an opportunity to see both sides of conditions like this," Jeeter continued, totally ignoring her comment. "When I am whole, I am pretty much accepted by other creatures great or small. But when I suffer disfigurement, I am observed with disgust and shunned by most although I am exactly the same individual."

Esther stared at the crustacean as he placed his complete arm with claw over the disfigured one as if to conceal it.

"How could any creature not notice this?" Jeeter sighed, surrendering to reality.

Esther began to move her mouth as if to speak but hesitated.

"Ask me anything, Esther. I will not be offended. Maybe you'll learn something."

Esther took a deep breath and looked searchingly into Jeeter's eyes.

"Do others make fun of you?"

"Yes," he muttered.

"Why would anyone do that? Do they think they are better than you?"

"Oh, it's not arrogance," Jeeter interjected, "but ignorance and fear. That's a behavior which hurts me much more than any physical ruin I experience."

"I am so sorry."

"Then there is pity!" Jeeter spoke harshly, striking a stare of disapproval,

Esther hung her head realizing she had exhibited just that.

"I don't want your pity," he said softly. "I just want to be included."

Esther felt strangely uneasy and could barely face the creature now.

"Esther!" he commanded the turtle's attention. "We all are missing something."

Esther glanced at the crayfish with apprehension.

"I sense you are missing something," he observed cautiously. "You are missing something not visible to the naked eye."

Esther lowered her head and released a deep sigh. A moment later she looked up and fixed her eyes on his.

"I am missing a piece of my heart," she whispered.

Jeeter tilted his head, twitched his feelers, and with a hint of a smile said, "I have good news for you, Esther."

She raised her chin attentively.

"Like my missing limbs, that too will heal," he assured her.

"Do you really think so, Jeeter?"

"If you really want it to be so," he answered with confidence. "Playing the victim never brought me any favors. Ponder your wound and address the true source."

"I wish I had a friend like you."

"Oh, I think you already do, Esther."

She blushed.

"Perhaps you should return home. Home is where your friends truly are."

"Friends?" Esther chuckled, shaking her painted head. "More like my enemies."

"Perhaps it's because you desire them to be so. Appearances

are deceptive, Esther. Often our ignorance creates monsters of individuals we truly do not know."

"If you say so," Esther mumbled sarcastically.

"Did you think of me as a monster when you first observed my disfigurement?"

"Like that matters now."

"It matters to me!" Jeeter snapped. "Suppose you hadn't bumped into me but saw my handicap from a distance. Would you have approached me to speak?"

"P-p-probably not," Esther stuttered.

"We all create barriers to protect us from things we don't understand. But often those walls become our prison of ignorance."

Jeeter limped up beside Esther.

An anxious Esther looked around her, restless to continue her journey.

"So where are you headed, Esther?"

"I am on a journey to find myself."

"I hope you will approve of who you find," Jeeter replied with a grin. "Is your journey driven by your disapproval with others, or are you really just unhappy with yourself?"

Esther cocked her head and stared into Jeeter's black eyes.

"I just want my life to be better."

"Better is what you make of it, Esther. It's a choice. I have every reason to be bitter, but I choose not to be."

Esther nodded with recognition.

"I think it would be better if you returned to the channel and seek healing for your broken heart there," Jeeter advised.

Esther swallowed hard and slowly shook her head a gentle *no*.

"I'm sorry, Jeeter, but I really must be on my way," she

announced as she began crawling away from the crayfish.

"Take care of yourself, Esther. I shall pray that you will heal." With that the crayfish limped back into the cove and descended below the surface of the mucky water.

Esther continued on her journey and soon came upon a sand dune that formed a bright wall of security along the shoreline. The water became shallow and Esther dipped her head beneath the surface as she paddled toward shore. She was amazed at the clean sandy bottom.

Esther was surprised when she noticed squiggly lines revealing a path along the bottom. *Doodles!* Esther remembered him with great excitement as she submerged and followed the meandering line.

She soon came upon a tip of shell rising just above the sand, signaling a creature buried beneath. Esther wedged her head under it and with a single thrust dislodged the object, flipping it backward onto the bottom surface. When the cloud of swirling sand settled, Esther could not believe her eyes.

"What business have you disturbing my sleep?" the creature grumbled.

"Uh-oh!" a startled Esther gasped. She stared at a highly irritated clam covered with a growth of silky weeds.

"Who are you?" the clam growled.

"I am Esther f-f-from the channel," she stammered, obviously embarrassed.

"Oh, one of the snobbish lot that is too good to be out here in the lake," the clam sneered. "You must think you are quite special, so full of yourself in that narrow little trench."

"I do not think of myself as special at all," Esther muttered. "Gack tells me I am, but I know I am more of a burden than a companion."

"What is a Gack?" the shellfish glowered.

"He is a bird, and he's really smart!"

"Birds! A vain bunch they all are," grumbled the clam.

Esther shook her head at the bitter creature in disagreement. "If you know so much, then perhaps I should know of you," she demanded.

The clam snaked out its tongue into the sandy bottom and crawled closer to Esther. Its shell twisted from side to side as slime drooled slowly from the corners of its jaw. Then the clam calmly spoke.

"I am Mumbles." He sidled up to Esther and brushed her shell inquisitively with his bristly tongue. "This Gack character," he sneered, "likely bosses you around, correct?"

"Well, sometimes it appears that way," Esther answered, "but I think his intentions are for my benefit."

"For your benefit?" scoffed the clam. "He's arrogant!"

Esther began to feel uncomfortable but kept her composure.

"You will find plenty of that nonsense out here. Have you met any of my fine neighbors out here?" he asked sarcastically.

"Well, Bull Beckett certainly was unpleasant," Esther shuddered. "He is very selfish."

"He's no joy, but he doesn't try to impress others."

"Madame Sweeney was very pleasant and wise, and Jeeter showed great compassion amid physical ruin."

"Sweeney? Jeeter?" Mumbles seethed. "That wrinkled wind bag and the limbless whiner? Those two are so full of themselves they sicken me."

Esther twisted up her face in anger and let out a hiss.

"Take that back!" Esther shouted. "They are my friends!"

"Then you are a loser, too!" growled the clam.

Esther swung her head with great fury into the creature,

sending it tumbling backward in a cloud of swirling sand.

"They are of more importance than you will ever be!" Esther shouted.

The clam came to rest on the bottom and straightened himself up with his bristly tongue.

"You are nothing today," Mumbles sneered, "and you will be nothing tomorrow, you worthless child."

Esther surfaced quickly and hurried to shore.

As she crawled up on the warm sand, a nearby bush rustled and out flew Gack. As usual he landed at Esther's side.

"You appear a bit frazzled, dear Esther," observed the red-winged blackbird. "Did it not go well with Madame Sweeney?"

"It's not Madame Sweeney who upset me!" an angry Esther replied. "Not Jeeter either."

"Jeeter?" Gack inquired.

"The crayfish I encountered. Have you never heard of him?"

"Not a Jeeter!" Gack exclaimed.

Esther broke into a wide smile and muttered, "Perhaps I will educate you about him and how to approach disfigurement someday."

A miffed Gack tapped his talons in the sand and raised an eyebrow.

"Err, please continue," Gack said, surrendering a grin.

"It was Mumbles who infuriated me so."

"Ah, yes," Gack said, nodding his head with recognition, "the jealous little clam."

"You know him?"

"I know *of* him," Gack responded in a despondent tone.

"He said you were arrogant," Esther told him reluctantly.

Gack cocked his head and ruffled his feathers up with irritation.

"You don't think you are better than me, do *you*, Gack?"

"My word, dear Esther!" crowed Gack. "I seem to recall it is *you* who can swim, not I."

"So, perhaps then," Esther snickered, *"you* are jealous of *me?"*

Gack began tapping his talons upon the sand again and raised both eyebrows.

"I *admire* you, Esther. Jealousy is Mumbles' game, not mine."

"Mumbles said Madame Sweeney was a wind bag," whispered Esther.

"Oh, he did, did he?" Gack cackled. "Can I assume he was equally unflattering about your new friend, Jeeter, as well?"

"Yes, quite so," she said striking a frown. "He even said I was a loser."

Gack began to cackle wildly but respectfully regained his composure.

"Sorry," Gack uttered. "I was not laughing at you, Esther. It's just that Mumbles is so strikingly petty. He desires to be the center of attention but does nothing to warrant it and resents those who receive it. He desires lower standards not high ambition."

"I don't quite get it, Gack."

"The achievements of others draw attention to his lack thereof. He is humiliated by this."

"But why would he not admire Madame Sweeney or Jeeter? They are no threat to him."

"To the contrary, dear Esther. Admiration is a mannerism for us who are confident in ourselves," Gack said, staring into Esther's bright yellow eyes. "When you believe in yourself, you are threatened by no one."

"He's bitter because no one pays him any attention, right?"

"He is bitter because he is a creature without merit," Gack explained. "Without merit of achievements, attention is fleeting."

"I am not an attention seeker," Esther stated and humbly bowed her head. "I would prefer to go unnoticed."

"You will never go unnoticed, dear Esther, because you are loved," Gack whispered. "I watch over you and so does Sir Elgin much to your disapproval. Boris may not speak with you, but he always displays a cordial smile. Even Bosco looks after you in his own twisted way. And, if you ever knew what was in Mr. Berig's heart. . . ."

Esther's eyes opened wide and then retreated to an unforgiving frown.

"We were talking about Mumbles," Esther reminded the blackbird.

"That we were," cackled Gack. "You are no loser, Esther, so pay no attention to what Mumbles said."

Esther straightened her neck and held her head up with dignity.

"Mumbles is just angry because others make him look bad?" she inquired.

"No, Esther!" Gack snapped. "It is Mumbles who makes himself look bad. He can blame no others for his misery."

"I guess you are right. Jeeter is disfigured, and he has every reason to be miserable, but he chooses not to be."

"By the grace of God, you have got it, Esther!" Gack crowed, striking a grin. "Now you see, Esther, that even misery can be a choice."

Gack slowly fanned his wings out and glanced at the sky above.

"I have pestered you enough," Gack announced with the wink of an eye. "This is your journey, Esther, not mine."

With that Gack lifted off in flight and vanished over the top of the bright enormous dune.

CHAPTER FIVE

ZIG ZAG, BROCK AND LORD SMYTHE

Esther stretched out her arms and legs and lay in the warm sun to ponder all she had encountered. Her thoughts were interrupted when she saw a rapid moving creature running up and down the shoreline just to her right. She recognized it as a sandpiper.

Esther amusingly observed the rapid pace of the bird back and forth as the creature drew closer. The bird was hunting for insects along the water's edge. Within just moments the bird was furiously darting in front of Esther kicking sand on her face.

"Pardon me," Esther grumbled, "but you're getting sand in my eyes!"

"I'm busy, busy, busy," reported the sandpiper.

Esther rattled her head, shaking the sand from her face.

The sound of chortling nearby surprised her, and she surveyed the surroundings to determine its origin. The brief scan was futile, so Esther redirected her attention back to the sandpiper.

"I am Esther from the channel." She scarcely said the words before another patch of sand brushed across her face. She began to spit sand from her mouth and impatiently added, "Who are you?"

The bird stopped abruptly and walked up to Esther. With its thin, straw-like beak, the bird blew the sand from Esther's face.

"I'm sorry about that," the sandpiper replied.

"Who are you?" Esther repeated.

"Zig Zag is my name," the sandpiper answered. "I've never seen you around these parts before, Esther. You say you come from the channel? I hear it's sort of an exclusive club."

Esther's mouth went agape. Not only did the creature walk fast; it talked so incredibly fast Esther barely understood a word it said.

"You sure are in a hurry!"

"Got to move or you lose! Of course, being a slow-poke as you are, you would not understand."

Esther released a low hiss which the hurried bird ignored.

Once again chortling nearby distracted her, and she turned her head in the direction of the sound, carefully examining the shoreline. Again she saw nothing.

"Just what are you doing out here in the lake?" Zig Zag asked.

"I am trying to find myself."

"I'm just trying to find some food," the sandpiper chuckled. "Perhaps if you moved a little faster, you would find yourself quicker."

"Very funny," Esther sneered.

"Just joking, but perhaps if you were more busy, you wouldn't have time to think of such silly things."

"Perhaps if you slowed your speech, others might be able to understand you."

"What-e-ver."

"Finding my identity is important to me."

"Well, you're a turtle." Zig Zag announced. "There's your identity. Now get over it!"

Esther began to tap her tail impatiently against the hot ground, and her heart began to pound with anger.

A third time the sound of chortling nearby caught Esther's attention.

"Where is that laughter coming from?"

"Oh, that?" Zig Zag observed with familiarity. "Over there?" the sandpiper asked, pointing his beak in the direction of a patch of dirt surrounded by beach grass.

Esther squinted and focused her yellow eyes.

Barely noticeable camouflaged by its surroundings was a very dark, dirty, plump toad half buried in the soil.

"That is Brock," Zig Zag scoffed.

Esther's squint increased but now with anger.

"Brock finds amusement at the expense of others," Zig Zag explained.

Esther sounded an alarming hiss in the direction of the fat toad.

"Care for a bug?" asked the sandpiper.

"No, thank you!"

"It's rather tasty," he added with a tempting grin.

"Not interested!"

"What-e-ver. I only stopped to be sociable. If you want to be antisocial, then so be it. I have bugs to catch, so I must be on my way."

With that the sandpiper continued its scurrying up and

down the shoreline foraging for food.

The bird's movements made her dizzy, so Esther decided to move on. She crawled up the shoreline in the direction of Brock, the toad.

She grimaced at the toad as she came upon him; Brock returned a surly grin.

"My identity is important to me," Brock mockingly sneered.

"Did you think that was amusing?" she snarled in response.

"Duh! Why do you think I was laughing?"

She shot a loathing glare at the creature.

"If you really want to see something funny," Esther scowled, "then you should look at your reflection in this lake sometime."

The toad snorted and struck a defensive posture.

"That was rude!"

"And you think it wasn't rude when you made fun of me?"

"Well, I do believe," Brock uttered sarcastically, "that you have a bit of sand on the tip of your nose."

"At least I'm not covered with dirt like you!" Esther sniped as she began to crawl on her way.

"That was not funny at all!" Brock bellowed.

Esther struck a wide grin and turned her head, spying the creature for one final volley. "If you enjoy making fun of others, you had best be prepared for others to make fun of you."

An unsettled Brock huffed and furiously dug deeper into the soil as if to conceal himself.

Just ahead along the shoreline, Esther spied a small wooded area and journeyed there to find shade. The sun had become so intense the surface of her shell was beginning to shed slightly. She briefly drank from the lake then continued to the woods.

The shade was welcome as Esther entered the small wooded area in search of food. She spotted the inviting green leaves of a bush and headed to them. But she stopped when she heard a faint cry.

"Help me! Help me!"

Esther peered about but saw nothing. Perhaps the heat of the day combined with the animated sandpiper and banter with the toad had, indeed, made her dizzy. She nuzzled the bush and pulled one of the luscious moist leaves from a vine, chewing it with delight.

"Help me! Help me!"

Esther tilted her head and stopped chewing. She looked around but again saw nothing. As she turned her attention back to the bush, out slithered a puff adder snake. Their eyes met, and the snake unleashed a nasty hiss and brought his head upright in a threatening manner.

"I'm not afraid of snakes," Esther muttered, staring at the creature.

The puff adder flattened its head to appear imposingly larger and darted its forked tongue from his mouth.

Ignoring the menace Esther picked another leaf from the bush.

"I am Lord Smythe," the puff adder exclaimed, "and this is my territory, so be gone with you!"

Esther kept a peripheral eye on the snake but didn't budge. The tension in the air was broken by a meek cry once again.

"Help me! Help me!"

The snake darted its forked tongue from his mouth, looked about, and said, "What is that?"

"I thought it was you," Esther replied in jest.

"What kind of deception is this?" Lord Smythe cried in anger as he crawled on the ground, his darting eyes surveying the surroundings.

Esther continued to feast but watched the snake as he

sniffed the air and tasted the breeze. Suddenly Lord Smythe came to an abrupt halt.

"Ah-ha! There we are," the puff adder declared with a contorted smile as it spotted a tiny water bug trapped in a spider's web. "Easy pickings," the snake sneered as it moved in closer.

"Help me! Help me!" the water bug cried out in panic.

Esther could not ignore the insect's impending fate. She reached inside of herself for courage. What she was about to do could have disastrous consequences.

Esther quietly crawled up behind the slithering menace, opened her mouth wide, grabbed the snake behind his head, and clamped down hard. Instantly the snake contorted his body and unleashed plowing recoil sending Esther tumbling backward and flipped her on her back.

"Take me for a fool, turtle?" Lord Smythe hissed. "Ponder your pathetic upside down world!"

The snake slowly slithered up to the spider's web as Esther extended her neck like an arm, plowing her head into the ground. She struggled furiously and gave a forceful thrust and flipped her body back upright upon the sand. This feat went unnoticed by the snake which was preoccupied with his impending snack.

"Say goodbye to your worthless existence," the snake sneered as he stared into the tiny water bug's eyes.

Esther quickly moved up to the snake's tail and bit down hard on it. The snake screamed in anger and looked back at Esther. She gave a sharp tug which sent the creature sliding backward and away from the web.

Lord Smythe reared upward, flattening his head.

"I am through with you, turtle!" Lord Smythe roared. "You just made a grave mistake!"

The snake bolted at Esther as she turned sideways and retreated inside of her shell. Lord Smythe's head bounced off the shell's hard surface with dizzying effect.

The enraged snake then methodically coiled its dusty gray-brown body around Esther tightly and began to squeeze with all his might but to no avail. Esther trembled inside.

She saw the snake's neck just outside of her shell. She quickly shot her head out, clamped down hard on Lord Smythe's neck once again and shook him violently. Lord Smythe let out a cry and tightened his grip. Twisting violently he was flipping and rolling the two of them again and again in the hot sand. Esther held on and would not let go.

Suddenly the puff adder became exhausted, and the two of them came to a rest. As quickly as it began, it was over. The snake released his grip on Esther, and in kind, she released Lord Smythe.

He shook his head and gave Esther a menacing gaze then slithered silently away in defeat.

A shaken Esther released a huge sigh and moved her arms and legs out from her shell, regaining her composure.

Esther turned around, found the spider's web, and slowly crawled near to have a look. Stuck in the center of the web was the trembling little water bug. Its shaky voice uttered but one thought.

"If you are going to eat me, please make it quick and be merciful!"

Esther opened her mouth wide and brought her head slowly up to the helpless insect.

CHAPTER SIX

COMPASSION
FOR ANOTHER

"I can't say I haven't been luckier than most in life," the bug shuddered, "but to be caught helpless like this is no luck at all."

Esther's mouth closed and her eyes widened.

"Now I'm going to do this again, OK?" said Esther.

She opened her mouth wide and put her nose in front of the bug.

"If you think I'm going to make lunch easy for you, you are crazy!" the insect said.

Esther drew her head back, closed her mouth again, and struck a frown.

"I'm not going to eat you!" Esther snipped. "I'm going to rescue you!"

"Sure you are," the bug sarcastically replied. "That's the oldest trick in the book, the old 'crawl in my mouth routine.'"

"I promise I will not eat you," an impatient Esther shouted. "I think water bugs are quite distasteful."

"Oh yeah," the insect scoffed, "it's bad enough I'm your afternoon snack, and now you insult me, too!"

Esther snorted and shook her wearisome head.

"If you don't grab onto my mouth the next time I open it before you, I may reconsider my tastes."

"Do you promise you will not eat me?" the bug shuddered.

"I promise!"

"Do you swear?" the insect added.

"I swear, I promise I will not eat you!" a fatigued Esther sputtered. "Now, please, grab onto my mouth and I will pull you free."

Esther opened her mouth wide once more and placed her face in front of the insect. The shuddering bug grabbed Esther's lower jaw and got a firm grip. Esther slowly began to draw back and the tiny creature, strand by strand, broke free from the spider's web.

"Put me down, put me down, please, please, please!" the insect cried hysterically as it swung from Esther's mouth.

Esther lowered her head to the ground. The bug released its hold and tumbled onto the sand.

"For crying out loud!" Esther shouted. "You are the most irritating creature I have ever met."

"I am sorry, your highness," the bug muttered, dusting itself off, "that I insulted your sincerity."

"It's OK. Forget it," and Esther rolled her eyes.

"No, I really, really, really mean it, your highness. I truly am most sorry," the insect squeaked as it bowed before the painted turtle.

"Stop it! You are embarrassing me."

"Whatever you say, big-hearted one. Can I call you that? Can

I, can I, can I?"

"NO! You are driving me crazy! Now be quiet!" Esther shouted.

The water bug put its front legs over its mouth as a gesture of silence and made not a sound.

"My name is Esther."

The water bug listened but stood motionless like a tiny statue.

"I come from the channel," Esther added, tilting her head, curiously spying the bug.

"And you?" She raised one eyebrow.

The bug remained silent.

"Do you have a name?" Esther began to impatiently thump her tail on the warm ground.

There was not a single peep.

"You can talk now!" Esther shouted totally frustrated.

"Well, there's really not much to say. My name is Skitters. I live out here in the lake. I have a brother named Twitters, a sister named Jitters, and a cousin named Quitters. He isn't a quitter, however. He is really quite ambitious and resourceful. He has his own pool of stagnant water and is greatly admired by pollywogs, tadpoles, and other scum dwellers."

Esther rolled her eyes again and began to slowly slip her head into her shell.

"Am I boring you?"

"Oh, my goodness," Esther mumbled, "why would you think that?"

"Some days I don't know when to shut up."

"No kidding!"

"Do you think I talk too much?"

"Well. . . ." Esther began.

"Well, do you, do you, do you?" Skitters rattled.

Ignoring the question Esther said, "I think I should be going now." She began to crawl away.

"Where are you going, Esther?"

Elsewhere, anywhere, Esther thought to herself.

The tiny water bug began to bounce after Esther.

"Can I come with you?"

"Well, I'm really rather busy."

"Doing what?" Skitters asked excitedly.

"Well," Esther hesitated, "I am trying to find myself."

"I once had an uncle who tried to find himself, and he got lost," Skitters commented very solemnly.

"I am not actually lost; I am just searching," was Esther's feeble attempt to explain.

"What you need is an assistant! Yes ma'am!" a cheerful Skitters told her and smiled broadly. "We will make a great team."

"We?" Esther was aghast.

"Yes! Won't it be awesome?"

A fatigued Esther began flipping her tail nervously.

"I really have no need for an assistant."

"I won't be any trouble."

Esther did not respond and continued down the shoreline back toward the cove.

"I promise I won't be any trouble really. I don't eat a lot, and my only vice is I snore when I sleep," a rejected Skitters called to her.

Esther did not respond and headed onward.

The spurned Skitters halted. He sat motionless in the hot sand as Esther moved on. His eyes filled with tears. He began to shake as if he were still caught in the spider's web and powerless to do anything.

Skitters raised his tiny face to the sky and opened his mouth and using his fragile voice cried with overwhelming anguish.

The tiny cry was so loud it created an echo.

Esther stopped dead in her tracks, but she hesitated to look behind her.

It seemed like a lifetime that she remained motionless, but it was mere seconds. Esther took a hard swallow. Then ever so slowly she began to turn her head back in the direction of Skitters.

The tiny creature was reduced to a pathetic sobbing ruin.

Esther released a huge sigh of defeat.

Skitters' eyes focused on Esther, and the two stared at each other.

He began to sob even more and unleashed an exaggerated screech of despair and thunderous sniffling thereby exploiting great drama.

Oh brother! Esther chuckled to herself, revealing a grin.

She looked up at the clouds, took a deep breath, and then refocused on the water bug, and mused, "I'm going to regret this."

"Come along," Esther said, "I'll take you with me."

Skitters bounced over to Esther rapidly with a look of amazement on his face. "You're not going to regret this," he sniffed breathlessly.

Esther kept her beak shut.

"Hop on to my back, and I'll carry you," Esther commanded.

There was the flutter of wings above, and Gack the red-winged blackbird touched down on the sand in front of Esther to block her way.

"Quite brave and touching, Esther," Gack observed. "It appears you have found a new friend."

"Well, sort of," she replied, rolling her eyes.

Aghast, Skitters backed up on Esther's shell a bit afraid.

"Is he going to eat me?" he inquired.

73

"No, this is Gack. Gack, this is Skitters."

"Well, it is a pleasure to meet you Skitters," Gack grinned. "That was quite a tussle you had back there with Lord Smythe, Esther."

"Yeah, and I won!"

"It appears," Gack said, winking at Esther's new companion, "you both did."

Esther was impatiently thumping her tail, Gack cleared his throat knowing it was time to leave.

"It appears you are headed back to the channel, I shall catch up with you there tonight."

He leaped into flight and soared off in the direction of the channel.

"He's my irritating, self-appointed guardian," Esther snorted, staring back at Skitters. "Let's be on our way."

Esther entered the water with Skitters riding piggyback and slowly paddled as she surveyed the scenery one last time.

"Before we leave the lake I want to say goodbye to Madame Sweeney," Esther muttered. "She's a wise elderly turtle."

Skitters, enjoying the ride, said nothing. The warm water rippled slowly around her as she navigated the cove. Hope filled her heart once again, and she stretched out her neck with joy.

Esther heard a sound overhead akin to a buzz, and a tiny voice followed.

"Headed back home, Esther?" the voice asked.

"Oh, Hector!" a surprised Esther said looking up in recognition. "Yes, I am returning to the channel."

Skitters observed the dragonfly suspiciously as it maneuvered in front of Esther's face striking a stationary flight.

"Back home to Bosco, the bullfrog," Esther sighed, "so he can spy on me and make my life miserable."

"Without reason no doubt," Hector sneered.

"Back to where Mr. Berig, the great blue heron, spends most of his days," Esther snarled. "He is the most arrogant creature you could ever meet."

"His day is coming, Esther," Hector assured the turtle. "He'll get his."

"And, back home to Sir Elgin, the blue racer snake," Esther scoffed. "The snitch!"

"Not to be trusted with secrets for sure." Hector agreed.

Skitters became alarmed with the chatter and wondered if Esther had any friends.

"I will leave you now," the dragonfly announced, "but continue to search for yourself, Esther."

Esther rolled her eyes and mumbled, "Yeah, right." Hector darted off and soon vanished from sight.

Esther continued on her way and zigzagged through the cattails and once again stopped briefly to smell the fragrant blooms atop the lily pads. In the distance the willow tree was gently waving in the light breeze.

"What's that old turtle's name again?" Skitters asked. "Who are we stopping to say goodbye to?"

"Madame Sweeney. She's a Blanding turtle."

"I once had a Blanding turtle try to eat me!" Skitters shuddered.

"You are my companion," Esther snickered. "She will not harm you."

An alarmed Skitters interrupted. "Esther, what is that in the water?"

Esther turned her head forward and fear gripped her.

"It's b-b-blood!" Esther stammered, observing the red-laced waters ahead.

"Oh my!" a shaken Skitters gasped. "Where is it coming from?"

Esther's eyes opened widely and a cold panic brushed over her.

"Madame Sweeney!" Esther screamed as she began to furiously swim in the direction of the willow tree.

Esther swam as hard as she ever had as both creatures anxiously surveyed the upcoming shoreline for signs of danger.

Skitters released a frightening scream. "Oh my goodness, Esther," Skitters cried. "What is that?"

Esther turned her head and caught a glimpse of a dark object to her left a short distance away upon the shoreline.

She drew her eyes into focus and could not believe what she saw.

"It's B-B-Bull Beckett!" Esther breathlessly sputtered.

The lifeless body of the bullhead lay on its side as gentle crimson waves washed against it.

Esther heard sobbing coming from under the willow tree and spotted a trembling Madame Sweeney hiding in the brush. Esther scrambled to her in a panic.

"Madame Sweeney, Madame Sweeney!" Esther cried. "Are you all right?"

There was no answer.

Esther drew up to her and began checking her over for wounds but found none.

Esther stuck her nose to Madame Sweeney's and whispered, "Are you OK?"

Overcome with grief, Madame Sweeney continued to sob. Esther crawled back to the cove and took water into her mouth and returned to sprinkle it on the elderly turtle's face.

"Madame Sweeney? Madame Sweeney?" Esther repeated.

"Are you all right?"

The ancient turtle finally responded gesturing a distressed nod of "yes."

Esther rubbed her neck up and down Madame Sweeney's wrinkled brow to comfort her. She also pulled a leaf from the brush and drew it softly over her friend's face to dry her tears.

All remained silent for some time. Finally a calm blanketed them, and Madame Sweeney settled down.

"Do you feel strong enough to speak?" Esther whispered.

Madame Sweeney nodded, cleared her throat, and uttered a broken "y-y-yes."

The wise old creature held her chin up, took a deep breath, and forced a composed smile.

"May I ask what happened here?" Esther anxiously inquired, looking down the shoreline at the lifeless wreckage of Bull Beckett.

"I-I-I was out in the cove floating as I dozed off. I was wakened by the sound of a boat occupied by men with spears."

Esther's eyes opened widely with recognition. She was sure it was the same men she had encountered earlier with Bull Beckett.

"I was doomed. At my age I don't have the strength to escape."

Skitters crawled closer to the front of Esther's shell, listening attentively.

"Then, suddenly, the waters beside the boat began to stir. It was Bull Beckett! He created a diversion by commanding the attention of the men."

Esther's mouth went agape, and she muttered, "What?"

"He afforded me the opportunity to escape. However," the elderly turtle recalled with anguish, "there was no escape for him."

Esther's heart felt a pinch as she hung her head in sorrow.

She simply could not believe what she had just heard. It made no sense.

Esther looked deeply into Madame Sweeney's ancient eyes with but one question on her mind.

"Madame Sweeney, why would Bull Beckett have done this?"

"Because, sweet Esther, Bull Beckett found his heart today."

The trio remained silent for some time comforting each other, and then Esther kissed Madame Sweeney on the cheek. She and Skitters bid the wise old turtle a solemn goodbye.

It was a hushed journey back to the channel as the sun began its descent toward the horizon. No words were spoken. Esther pondered all she had heard and witnessed out in the lake that day. Slowly, promise was beginning to build inside once again.

She knew if Bull Beckett could find his heart there was hope for her.

CHAPTER SEVEN

THE JOURNEY
BACK HOME

As Esther entered the mouth of the channel, anxiety brushed over Skitters and the tiny creature began to talk.

"What's the scoop on life here in the channel?" he asked hesitantly.

"What do you mean?"

"Who should I watch out for?"

"Oh, I understand. This is all about being eaten again, right?"

"Hey!" bellowed Skitters. "I don't have a cozy shell I can retreat into. I'm everyone's potential snack!"

Esther looked to her rear and snickered at the tiny creature riding piggyback on her shell.

"Well, what's the dirt here?" Skitters mumbled.

"I don't know everyone in the channel, but I am familiar with most. If you mind your own business, it's a safe place."

"Do you have any enemies here, Esther?"

"Well, I despise Mr. Berig, the great blue heron."

"What did he do to you?"

"Well, that's sort of a long story. Bosco, the bullfrog, is nasty and always has something sarcastic to say, but otherwise he is harmless. However, he does eat bugs."

Skitters shuddered and took a small gulp.

"I have issues with Sir Elgin, the blue racer snake," Esther shared, "but he's always civil."

"It doesn't sound too dangerous here, except for that frog."

"Bosco?" Esther nodded. "But you should find it peaceful here."

After a brief pause, Skitters continued his inquiry. "Why did you leave to come out into the lake? It's much more dangerous out there. Is there something about the channel you are not telling me?"

"The channel is unsettled but only for me."

"Oh, that explains a lot," Skitters commented sarcastically.

"It's personal," Esther grumbled.

Skitters pondered that thought then asked, "Do you have any friends here, Esther?"

"Well," Esther replied very slowly as if she were not quite positive what to say or if she even wanted to answer. "You've met Gack, the red-winged blackbird. Gack is my friend, always has been since I was a baby."

"And?" he asked as he tapped his legs on Esther's shell eager to hear more.

"Oh, there's Boris, the otter," Esther added. "Yes, Boris. We've never exchanged a single word, but we cross paths often, and we always trade cordial smiles."

"And?" Skitters inquired further.

"I once met a snail I considered to be my first friend," Esther mumbled. "His name was Doodles, but I haven't seen him since I was a baby."

"Anyone else?" the water bug persisted.

"I have," Esther said with a solemn sigh, "or had, a secret friend once."

"I like secrets!" Skitters was so excited he squeaked, "Who was it?"

"It was private, OK?" Esther grumbled. "I'd rather not discuss it."

There was a long pause. Skitters waited to hear about more creatures, but no other names were offered.

"Doesn't sound as if you have many friends."

"I pretty much keep to myself." Esther was getting agitated.

"Well, at least you have me," Skitters responded gleefully.

"Don't remind me."

Esther stopped paddling and slowed as the gentle current drew them near to the shambles of the structure known as Termite Bridge.

"This is where you get off," Esther ordered.

"What?" Skitters cried. "You're going to leave me?"

"I live alone," she answered tersely. "You will be safe here."

Skitters began nervously checking the surroundings.

"You'll be safe. Besides, I live just down the channel. If something comes up, just come to my log."

"I'm scared, Esther," said a trembling Skitters.

Esther stuck her nose to the creature's face and whispered, "You will be just fine here, really."

"How do I know you're not just abandoning me? How do I know you even have a log just beyond this bridge?"

"Because I told you I do," Esther said patiently.

"I guess I believe you," he said with hesitation.

"You can visit me tomorrow, OK?"

Esther crawled up on the shore, and Skitters bounced off of her back to the ground. The tiny bug's eyes immediately filled with tears.

"It is safe here by Termite Bridge," Esther spoke in a reassuring tone.

"I g-g-guess so," the tiny creature stammered, staring down the channel. "You say your log is that way?"

"Yes, just beyond this bridge."

"Then I can visit you tomorrow for sure?"

"Yes! You can visit me tomorrow."

"Promise, promise, promise?" squeaked Skitters.

Esther shook her head as she turned around and crawled back into the channel.

"Do you promise?" Skitters shouted in panic.

She groaned. "Yes, I promise, promise, promise!"

A relieved Skitters stood by the shoreline with a tiny grin on his face and waved goodbye.

When Esther had just passed Termite Bridge, she heard a soft flutter of wings. The sound was too gentle to be Gack.

Esther looked above and saw a beautiful Monarch butterfly approaching her.

"Hello, Esther!" the Monarch announced as it darted over Esther's head and proceeded up the channel.

That was odd! I don't know a butterfly, Esther pondered. *How would that creature know my name?*

Esther shrugged off the encounter as she continued paddling down the channel. *Much stranger things have happened to me today,* she assured herself.

Esther began to look about her as she swam on, and the

familiar surroundings were comforting. It was good to be home.

She could see her log and slowly swam to it.

There was a sudden thrust of fury above. Mr. Berig was passing overhead heading downstream.

"Evil creature," the painted turtle muttered as she pulled herself onto her log.

Esther surveyed her log and scratched her claws into its surface as if to reclaim and mark her territory. Suddenly she felt a rush of wind above her and the unmistakable tap sound of claws touching down on the parched bark.

It was Gack paying Esther a visit. "Hello, dear Esther."

"You again?"

"Well!" Gack sputtered.

When she saw the serious look in the red-winged blackbird's eyes, her attitude changed. "Sorry."

"Word has spread quickly over the demise of Bull Beckett. I spoke with Madame Sweeney moments ago, and she informed me you were there. Are you all right, Esther?"

"It was awful the way he died. It was so sad." She spoke softly.

"Fact is, Esther, the saddest thing of all is that few will miss him."

Esther closed her eyes and bowed her head.

"Few know how Bull Beckett perished. Few care to know." Gack tapped his talons on Esther's log and added, "They're just glad he's gone."

"Well, I'm not."

"It seems the courageous act that ended his life should be an epitaph of who he was. Unfortunately, he will be remembered only as a monster."

Esther released a shattered sigh of grief.

"This should serve notice to us all," Gack said imposingly, "to consider how we wish to be remembered."

"It's not fair. Saving Madame Sweeney should have changed all that," muttered Esther.

"But it didn't!" Gack replied. "A lifetime of selfish behavior simply overwhelmed an admirable ending."

"Sad," whispered Esther.

"Sad, indeed," Gack answered. "But he who created Bull Beckett wanted to lift that burden from him and forgive him."

"Do you mean God?" Esther whispered.

"He created us all," replied Gack. "You were shaped from the same clay as Bull Beckett. It is only your choices in life that make you different."

"He is forgiven though?"

"Our creator is always forgiving. All we need do is accept him and his forgiveness, dear Esther. He loves us all even if we are not so forgiving to one another."

Esther rested her head upon her log and pondered Gack's comments.

"You know, Gack?" Esther said in a sullen voice. "Part of me wishes I could have become friends with Bull Beckett."

"It was his choice, not yours."

"I really tried," Esther sighed. "He just would not accept me no matter what I did."

"Oh, dear Esther, do you realize we spend a great amount of our time trying to please or become accepted by others. Often it is to no avail. If we keep spending time to impress others, do you know what happens?"

"No," she said timidly.

"Well, if we concentrate on that, we waste the few moments we have with those we love and those who love us."

Esther looked deep into the blackbird's eyes and smiled.

"Some will never accept us, Esther, so why should our thoughts allow them so much of our attention?" Gack questioned. "They are the ones who are unhappy. Must we be unhappy, too?"

"I am unhappy at times. There are certainly some creatures I cannot accept. In fact, some just make me angry," Esther admitted while trying to justify her feelings. "But I have reasons for being angry!"

"Anger has little to do with reason," Gack insisted. "Have you ever imagined mending your differences with Mr. Berig as an example?"

"He's arrogant," Esther snarled.

"A claim likewise tagged upon me by Mumbles the clam," Gack cackled. "A falsehood would you not agree?"

Esther rolled her eyes in reluctant agreement. "I just wish there was a way to fix the problems that exist here in the channel."

"Are all of the problems yours to fix?"

"Some of them."

"Then leave what is left for the others to fix. Address only what you can," he advised.

"You do have a way of fixing problems," Esther said with admiration.

"You may imagine so. I often get between conflicts, but I assure you I resolve nothing. That choice belongs to those in conflict."

"It would appear otherwise."

"But that is an illusion, Esther. It is like when I stood on your shell and allowed you the appearance of flight reflected on the channel's surface," he explained. "In reality not all wish to witness a reflection of what they truly are."

"But how can I ever forgive others for what they have done to me?" Esther mumbled.

"You simply forgive them!" Gack crowed.

"Surely even you would say forgiveness would have to be mutual," she declared.

"In an ideal existence, y-y-yes," he sputtered. "Everyone has unresolved issues, Esther. Some will never surrender their anger because they find strange comfort in it. To let go of that burden may be an admission of guilt, and they do not wish to believe that they are wrong, too!"

"I'm not sure I'm ready to forgive anyone," exclaimed Esther.

Gack shook his feathered crown with disappointment.

"It is something to dream about though," Esther sighed.

"And dreams are always within reach, dear Esther," whispered Gack.

Esther nodded her head in agreement.

Gack cleared his throat and changed the subject. "My dear Esther, did you find yourself out in the lake?"

"No," Esther disclosed her disappointment. "Hector was wrong."

"Hector, the agreeable little dragonfly?"

"Don't tell me you know him, too!" said a surprised Esther.

"Esther, Hector is anything but straightforward." Gack continued to express his disapproval. "He cannot be taken seriously."

"He seemed very sympathetic to my situation," a defensive Esther replied.

"Hector has a bad habit of telling others what they want to hear."

"I have to disagree. Hector understood my grievances with Bosco, Mr. Berig, and Sir Elgin."

"My word, dear Esther!" Gack crowed. "It's unlikely that

Hector knows any of them."

"Well, I did like what I heard."

"What else did Hector tell you?"

"He said that if I left the channel I would leave my troubles behind."

Gack shook his feathered crown with dismay and cackled gently.

"Esther, let me tell you something about friendships. Creatures who only tell you what you want to hear do you no favors. Only true friends will have the courage to tell you what you need to hear even if you should disapprove."

Esther reluctantly nodded her head in agreement.

"Well, Esther, if you didn't find yourself while out in the lake, may I ask what you brought back from that experience?"

"Skitters!"

Gack cackled gently.

"I brought Skitters into the channel and dropped him off at Termite Bridge. No doubt that creature will present a challenge for me."

"But it was your choice to bring him into the channel, correct?" Gack responded with a grin.

Esther nervously thumped her tail on her log.

"That water bug is going to drive me crazy, Gack. I'm not sure it was in my best interest to bring him here."

"In *your* best interest?" crowed Gack. "It was not in Bull Beckett's best interest to save Madame Sweeney, but it was the right thing to do."

"You don't understand, Gack."

"Oh, don't I?" Gack responded, ruffling up his feathers. "Perhaps I should have imagined the same thing when I saved your life, Esther. Should I have concluded that it would not be in my best interest to become your friend?"

Esther suddenly struck a look of embarrassment.

"I guess I will just have to see where my relationship with that water bug goes."

"Esther," Gack addressed her in a hushed tone, "you did the right thing by Skitters. Doing the right thing is always in your best interest."

Esther fixed her yellow eyes up at the fragile clouds now brushed with colors. Gold and crimson hues began to flicker across the green water of the channel as the sun set behind the trees.

Esther turned to Gack, "This day is done."

"And, dear Esther, tomorrow is a new one and full of choices." Gack lifted into the sky and flew off over the treetops.

Esther stretched out her arms and legs and rested her chin on her log. She watched Boris, the otter, swim by on the way to his dwelling, and then Bosco, the bullfrog, passed, giving Esther a routine glare.

Esther's eyes began to become heavy and she released a wide yawn. She struggled to stay awake but to no avail. She closed her eyes and let go.

Darkness suddenly swept over her, and the sound of flowing water began to ring in her ears. A bright light flashed and suddenly everything was drawn into focus.

Esther was dreaming again.

She was a baby once again.

She was exiting the wreckage of her forbidden playground, the submerged yellow rowboat, and headed to the water's surface.

The voice of Doodles the snail came into her head and his words, "If I should never see you again, Esther, I do hope all of your dreams come true."

When Esther surfaced, she noticed she was slightly down the channel from the bow of the boat. She began to swim upstream toward it but to no avail. Her tiny body struggled in the current as she slowly began moving backward.

As the gentle channel current carried Esther, she stopped paddling and surveyed her surroundings. She had never been this far downstream. She observed snowy clusters of Queen Anne's lace and golden spotted touch-me-nots along the rich green shoreline. She smiled and her tiny bright yellow eyes twinkled with excitement.

An otter swam past her headed downstream. It was the otter baby Esther saw routinely near her home, but she didn't know his name.

Downstream in the distance she heard a roar and a rumble which echoed up the channel like thunder. Upstream in the distance Esther spied her mother paddling furiously toward her.

"Esther!" her mother called out. "Swim to the channel bank!"

Esther looked confused as she saw no danger.

The tip of the rowboat vanished from view as baby Esther rounded a bend in the channel. The current tightened its grip.

"Swim to the channel bank as quickly as you can!" her mother shrieked in horror.

Esther began to paddle toward the bank, but the current became more rapid. She twisted and turned struggling to regain her balance.

Suddenly a repeated "caw" sound reported overhead.

Tiny Esther looked up and observed a perched red-winged blackbird looking downward from a tree branch over the channel. The anxious bird began pacing its branch observing Esther with panic.

"Swim to the bank!" Esther's mother screamed.

The thunderous roar began to build and fill the air drowning out the alarming cries of Esther's mother and the panicked cawing of the blackbird.

Suddenly there was a bright flash of light then all went black.

Esther woke and she was sweating profusely.

She shook her head violently and looked upward expecting to see a blackbird, but instead she saw the moon and flickering stars in a deep ebony sky.

The melodic sound of crickets echoed a peaceful nighttime backdrop.

She was safely on her log.

Her nightmare was over.

A chill ran through her and she took a deep breath.

She laid her head back on her log and muttered, "Please, dear God."

A calm brushed over Esther like a warm blanket. Her eyelids lowered slowly and she released a gentle sigh. Darkness filled her mind's eye and a bright image began to glow gracefully. It was Esther's mother. At that very moment, Esther let go and slipped into a peaceful slumber.

CHAPTER EIGHT

THE VANISHING CHANNEL

Billowy fog crawled slowly over the still green water of the channel as the first hint of a rising sun announced the beginning of a new day.

Slowly creatures began to wake from peaceful slumber, and the waters of the channel began to gently ripple with movement.

With the break of dawn, Boris, the otter, was one of the first creatures to traverse the water. His work began early. Boris gathered floating sticks to add to his humble dwelling, a dwelling that was meticulously rebuilt daily.

The activity in the channel was routine and mundanely familiar, but something about this morning was different. Gack, the red-winged blackbird, was the first to notice it.

Today would be anything but routine.

Gack was so concerned about it that he urgently landed atop

Esther's log earlier than usual to wake the creature.

"Esther, dear Esther, do wake up!" Gack crowed.

The turtle stuck only her tiny nostrils and drowsy eyes out from her shell and unleashed a wide yawn.

"Good morning to you, Esther," Gack cheerfully announced to the wakening turtle.

Esther slithered her entire head out from her shell with her eyes a squint to shield her from the sun's bright reflection on the water. Then she stared half conscious at Gack.

"It is very early, so this had better be important," Esther scowled.

"How about a good morning?" Gack demanded impatiently, tapping his talons upon Esther's log.

"OK! Good morning, Gack," Esther grumbled. "Now what do you want?"

"For some reason the channel is going dry, dear Esther," Gack explained.

"That's nice and have a good day." She scoffed and retreated back into her shell.

A frustrated Gack hopped upon Esther's back and began to tap his attention-compelling beak on her painted turtle shell.

"Hello, is there anyone home?" he bellowed.

Esther's head shot out from her shell, and she released a nasty hiss.

"OK, suit yourself, but don't say I didn't alert you," Gack warned, shaking his feathered crown as he lifted off into flight.

"Hey, wait! I'm sorry."

But Gack was gone.

"You never listen, do you?" a raspy voice accused.

Esther snaked her head to her right and gliding toward her was Bosco, the bullfrog. She rolled her eyes and prepared for a hassle.

"What do you want?" Esther said flippantly.

"Gack is correct, you disobedient fool," the bullfrog sneered.

Esther drew back her head and returned completely inside her shell to ignore the creature. She loathed the bullish frog.

"Best move on, girl, before your log is sitting high and dry," Bosco chuckled.

Esther glared at the frog as it glided by her.

She blinked her sleepy eyes and surveyed the channel. She was uncertain if the claims were true. The appearance of the water and shoreline landmarks seemed unchanged.

Esther shrugged and was about to draw her head back into her shell to continue her sleep when she heard a familiar gentle flutter of wings.

"Hello, Esther!" a fragile voice greeted her.

Esther looked up. Flying above her was the beautiful Monarch butterfly she had encountered upon returning to the channel last evening.

This time, however, the creature did not pass overhead but instead landed on the log beside her.

"Sorry I didn't stop yesterday." The butterfly was very timid and Esther struck a clueless glare at the tiny creature.

"I was trying out my new wings," the Monarch explained as she fanned out her wings in display.

Esther forced a polite smile and responded slowly, "H-h-how do you know my name?"

"That's funny, Esther," the butterfly snickered.

Esther struck an aloof posture and softly uttered, "I beg your pardon, but I do not believe we have ever met."

Much to Esther's surprise, the butterfly hopped up and landed on the tip of her nose. The creature's eyes sparkled as she displayed a strangely familiar grin.

"Really, Esther," the butterfly scoffed. "Stare deep into my eyes."

Esther's mouth suddenly went agape with recognition.

"Oh goodness!" Esther gasped. "No way!"

"No way?" the butterfly snickered. "Esther, I am your secret friend."

Esther's bright yellow eyes opened wider than they had ever been before.

"Dee Dee?" Esther whispered.

"Yes!" the butterfly snickered. "It's me!"

Dee Dee then hopped from Esther's nose and gently landed by her side once again.

"My word!" an astounded Esther said, twisting her head. "What happened to you? I thought you were dead."

"Dead?" Dee Dee giggled as she fanned out her angelic-like wings. "No, Esther, I was born again."

"But, w-w-what of that trap I saw you motionless within?" stammered Esther.

"The chrysalis?" Dee Dee chuckled. "I was compelled to make that cocoon, Esther, and when I emerged from it, I was transformed."

Esther twisted up her face. She could not comprehend the miraculous metamorphosis. Then she released a gentle sigh of relief and pushed her nose up closely to Dee Dee and nudged the creature with compassion.

"I missed you Dee Dee." A single tear rolled down her painted cheek.

Dee Dee gently brushed one of her soft orange wings aside of Esther's cheek to dry her tear and whispered back, "Esther, I never left."

Esther swallowed hard and blinked to regain her composure.

"Yesterday I experienced a miraculous transformation," Dee Dee explained. "I have a feeling today will be your turn."

Esther smirked with amusement and shrugged with disbelief.

"Oh really?" snorted Esther. "Will God be giving me the wings I have always dreamed of?"

"No, Esther," the butterfly chuckled.

"Then what creature will I be changing into?" she asked in jest.

"Your miraculous transformation will not be one which changes your outer appearance, Esther. The change will occur deep within you."

Esther looked at Dee Dee with apprehension.

"Today, my secret friend, that broken heart of yours will become whole once again," Dee Dee spoke with such assurance. She lifted off and hovered briefly in front of Esther's face. "Oh, and Esther, the channel is going dry."

Esther's secret friend graciously fluttered away. After surveying the area, Esther slid from her log and into the channel. The drop to the water was noticeably farther. The channel was indeed lower. A startling thought came over her. "This may be my last opportunity to journey to the dam."

The last half-mile of the channel, before it entered Lake Michigan, was blocked by a large steel dam. For years it had regulated the level of Silver Lake that fed the small waterway. The dam had been abandoned long ago and suffered from disrepair. It had neither been lowered nor raised in years.

Knowledge of the dam was rare in the channel, and it was shrouded in mystery.

Very few water creatures ventured there for the monstrous dam was hazardous. Many, swept away by its unforgiving current, had perished traversing over the great structure to the rocks below. Only birds and land creatures could observe the dam in safety and report on it.

So it was, with great courage, that Esther began her way to the dam that incredible morning.

No doubt she would encounter Mr. Berig there standing like an arrogant sentinel. The great blue heron often fished at the dam.

Esther's eyes were opened wide and her breathing became anxious. An icy chill gripped her in the comforting warm green waters as she began to paddle downstream.

She had to return to a memory which had tormented her. It ravaged her with guilt, regret, shame, and anger. She was seeking her past to resolve her future.

Concern washed over Esther as she paddled down the channel. Great branches which she previously had seen underwater now beckoned above the surface. The shoreline had expanded too. The channel, no doubt, was noticeably narrower than the day before.

"Where you going, where you going?" a nervous little voice sounded.

Esther reared her head to glimpse Skitters bouncing effortlessly atop the water.

"Hello, Skitters," she said aloofly.

"What are up to?" Skitters could never hide excitement.

"Just checking stuff."

"Where are you headed?" the water bug persisted.

"Of what business is that of yours?" Esther replied tersely.

Skitters glided alongside in silence.

"Sorry, I was just checking out the water level." It was Esther who broke the silence.

"Then it's true?" the water bug asked.

"What is true?" the turtle said impatiently.

"That the channel is drying up, and we're all going to die!" Skitters cried.

"Nonsense! Perhaps some fish will die, but we legged and flying creatures can find a new home."

"Then the c-c-channel is drying up?" Skitters stammered.

"Look around and see for yourself," the turtle said as she surveyed the increasing shoreline.

"Where are you going?" Skitters persisted with excitement in his squeaky voice.

"If you must know, I'm headed to the dam," Esther answered impatiently. "Look, don't you have somewhere else you could be now?"

Skitters easily ignored Esther's negative attitude. "A dam? What's a dam? It sounds exciting! Can I come with you? Please, please, please?"

Esther gave Skitters a long glare. She felt responsible for the little creature. She recalled her childhood and knew what it was like to be rescued from certain death. She understood the bond that can form between two creatures fostered from crisis. So with some reluctance Esther approved of Skitters tagging along.

"Well, OK, but be quiet. Don't talk unless I talk to you. Understood?" Skitters kept his mouth shut. Esther did observe that the little water bug bounced a little higher on the surface of the water immediately upon notice of his inclusion.

The sun had come into full view, clearing the treetops, when Esther saw a rapid wake just below the surface of the water approaching. She stuck her head under and opened her yellow eyes.

It was Boris, the otter.

The creature circled rapidly before surfacing.

Esther raised her head.

"I checked the dam and it's stable. The problem has to be at the inlet upstream at Silver Lake," announced an out of breath Boris.

Esther nodded, but she and Skitters continued to go forward.

"Don't go there, Esther!" Boris appealed. "It's unsafe!"

"I'll be OK."

Strange, Esther thought. *That's the first time the two of us have ever spoken.*

"How unsafe is it, huh, huh, huh?" Skitters excitedly asked Boris.

"Don't speak unless you are spoken to, understood?" Esther reminded the water bug. Then she turned to the otter to offer a thank you, but it was too late. Boris was already darting upstream.

Esther and Skitters came upon a submerged, yellow, wooden rowboat which rose slightly above the surface. It resembled a rotten skeletal frame.

"My forbidden childhood playground," Esther sighed, looking at the remains. "When I was a baby, I used to swim inside of this wreck much to my mother's disapproval."

"A boat is supposed to be something that is underwater?" Skitters inquired.

"Well, actually, a boat is supposed to be above water," Esther explained.

"Oh! Well, then, how did it get underwater?" he asked with great curiosity.

"You are testing my patience! Just be quiet, OK?" Esther replied.

At that moment the current picked up slightly, and the boat twisted loose from its grave and began to tumble half afloat down the channel as it passed them.

"This, my little friend, is where we should part ways," Esther said with concern. "The more shallow the water becomes the faster the rapids will flow to the dam."

"I could ride on your back," Skitters suggested, displaying a shrug.

Esther gave the creature a glance of uncertainty.

"All right, hop on. But if the rapids become too hazardous, I let you off at the bank, understood?" the turtle warned.

Skitters nodded and hopped up on Esther's shell.

Esther refocused. She tried to recall how far the dam was beyond where the old rowboat had been. It had been a long time, and it was only a fragmented vision from her childhood. She had only a few memories from then. Few she cared to remember.

The channel current had slowed as Esther and Skitters entered a widened area of the waterway.

"Why are you going to the dam?" Skitters questioned.

"I thought we had an agreement. No talking."

She had wasted her breath. Skitters was unstoppable. "I mean if the channel is going dry, the secret to why lies behind us not ahead of us."

The turtle said nothing.

"Boris said there's nothing wrong with the dam!" Skitters continued.

Esther stopped paddling and impatiently began thrashing her tail in the water.

Skitters still pressed. "If the dam isn't the reason for the drop in the water level, why go there?"

"I think I know why," a voice came from overhead.

A startled Esther and Skitters looked above to see Sir Elgin, the blue racer snake, clinging from a branch over the channel.

"Why don't you tell your little friend why, Esther?" the snake hissed.

"Stay out of this, Sir Elgin," Esther scowled.

"I recall you making a pledge once to me and to Gack," Sir Elgin said while uncoiling from the branch into the water. "You pledged that you would never pass this way again."

Esther turned her head trying to shun Sir Elgin. Skitters was confused and a bit frightened by the snake.

"Your little companion is right," Sir Elgin continued. "The channel disappearing has nothing to do with the dam. You just don't want to see a memory fade away before the water stops flowing over it."

"Shut up!" Esther snapped.

"Maybe it's not my place," Skitters began.

Esther twisted her head back and shouted, "It's not your place, and it's none of your business!"

Sir Elgin slithered ahead of the turtle and began to swim like a flowing blue ribbon, rippling the water in front of Esther as if to block her way.

"I know what you're thinking, Esther," Sir Elgin said contentiously. "But trust me. Going to the dam will resolve nothing."

"Move aside, Sir Elgin!" Esther shouted.

Sir Elgin gave Esther another hiss then moved aside adding, "Do not make the same mistake twice, Esther."

Esther continued to paddle forward.

Skitters was shaken over the encounter.

"Can I just say one thing?"

"No!" Esther snapped.

Suddenly the remains of the old yellow rowboat caught Esther's eye. Skitters, too, noticed the ruin now resting along the channel's bank.

"Esther, where is your mother?" he asked.

Esther released a sigh. She was silent.

"When you mentioned playing underwater inside of that boat, that was the first time I've ever heard you mention her," the water bug said with curiosity.

Skitters noticed Esther couldn't take her eyes off the wooden wreck as they slowly passed by.

"That boat brings back something painful?" he inquired in a solemn voice.

"Yes, it does," Esther sighed.

Skitters then mustered up the courage to ask, "Is your mother, um . . . dead?"

Esther hesitated. Then in a mournful manner she spoke, "Yes, she died when I was only three weeks old."

"Have you ever been this far down the channel before?"

"Only once. When I was three weeks old," Esther whispered.

Skitters became silent not knowing what to think or if it was wise to ask anything further.

Esther's breathing had become heavy.

Perhaps this was a good time for Skitters to stay quiet.

CHAPTER NINE

CONFRONTING THE PAST

As they entered a narrow stretch of the channel, the current began to pull a little more.

Skitters stretched out on Esther's back. Esther straightened her head in a dignified fashion and regained her composure.

Esther had just released an anxious sigh when she heard wings beating with fury overhead.

It was Mr. Berig, the great blue heron, no doubt flying to the dam in search of something to eat.

"He stood there and did nothing," Esther grumbled with anger while she observed the creature in flight.

"Excuse me?"

"Mr. Berig! I hate that creature!" Esther sputtered as Skitters looked up, catching a glimpse of the blue heron before it disappeared behind the treetops.

"You mean that big bird?" Skitters inquired.

Esther nodded her head with contempt.

"What did he do?"

"Nothing!" Esther bristled. "He did absolutely nothing!"

"Not a reason to dislike someone, really," Skitters announced bravely. "I can understand if they did something, but if they didn't?"

"He let my mother die, and I shall never forgive him for that."

Suddenly, a jolt went through Esther's body, as if she had been slapped from above. She turned her head and released an alarming hiss that sent a frightened Skitters tumbling off into the channel.

"Still in a bad mood, Esther?"

It was Gack, the red-winged blackbird.

He had imposingly perched himself atop Esther's shell.

"Kind of wobbly, aren't we?" Gack cackled as the unstable turtle teetered with the additional weight.

Esther grumbled at the intrusion.

"Going somewhere you shouldn't, Esther?" Gack asked, as Skitters scampered back atop Esther and scurried to get comfortable beside Gack.

"Skitters, how nice to see you," Gack said striking a pleasant smile. "By chance, would you two be headed to the dam?"

"Why, yes, but, I don't know why," Skitters answered with confusion while shaking water from his ears.

"I trust Esther knows by now that the channel going dry has nothing to do with the dam being compromised. Would that be correct?" inquired Gack.

"Oh, she knows," Skitters began to say.

"Shut up," Esther muttered.

"I seem to recall, Esther, when you were just three weeks old, that you made me and Sir Elgin a promise. Would you recall what that promise may have been, Esther?" Gack inquired.

Esther bit her hooked lip, then muttered, "Yes, I recall."

"Then why are you traveling to that place again, dear Esther?" he asked with a disapproving tone.

There was no answer.

"You know the waters will soon drop lower than the dam's spillway, and the current will no longer traverse over it. Esther, is there some need to relive that day? Is there perhaps a desire to feel what she must have gone through?" he probed.

Esther's squinted eyes and chilling silence confirmed Gack's suspicion.

"So that's it," Gack shook his feathered crown. "Esther, fair warning. Beware when you seek the truth, you may not like what you find."

Esther stuck her head underwater. She had no desire to hear any more of this. When she resurfaced, she was scowling.

"I have done a little tree hopping, Esther. I've been keeping tabs on your journey, and I do not like what I see." scolded Gack.

"You don't understand!" Esther snapped.

"I understand enough. I understand that you still harbor ill feelings toward Sir Elgin for telling your mother that day," he continued. "You also foolishly hold Mr. Berig responsible."

"Yeah, right." Esther sneered.

"Do not take that tone of voice with me, Esther!" Gack warned. "It was I who saved your life that day."

The conversation came to an abrupt end for breaking through the silence there came a sound.

It was a deep sound.

It was a tumultuous rumble.

It was a sound like thunder.

Gack leaped into flight, and suddenly Esther became quite unsettled.

"Perhaps you should reconsider the promise you made to Sir Elgin and Gack?" a shuddering Skitters suggested. "Whatever that was."

"Whatever it was doesn't concern you."

"It must have to do with going this far downstream," Skitters observed. "It has to do with the dam, right?"

"I do not intend to take you with me the entire way," grumbled Esther. "Why is this of any concern to you?"

"Well," he whimpered, "you're kind of my friend."

"Kind of?" Esther mumbled.

"Well, maybe I care about what happens to you."

"Well, maybe you shouldn't."

"Sir Elgin was nothing like Lord Smythe," observed Skitters. "He seems to care about you, and he didn't even attempt to eat me."

Esther flinched. "There you go again with your obsession about being eaten."

"Why don't you just keep the promise you made to those two and just turn back? It's not too late."

"Oh, but it is."

"Gack and Sir Elgin think it's not."

"Gack thinks he's my mother, and Sir Elgin is a tattle tale." Esther replied.

"Sir Elgin is a tattle tale? Sir Elgin told whom what?"

"Sir Elgin is partially responsible for what happened to my mother."

"I don't see how a tattle tale could k-k-kill anyone," the insect stammered.

"I told you when I brought you to the channel that this place is unsettled for me. None of this concerns you."

Skitters looked up as they began to round a bend in the channel. His beady black eyes squinted. He could not yet see the dam, but the vicious, destructive roar of it was unmistakable.

"This is where you get off," Esther announced, arching her neck back, staring at the water bug.

Skitters was shaking as his excitement quickly turned to fear.

"I'll drop you off at the bank," Esther shouted over the roar of the dam.

Her swimming was labored due to the current, but the waters calmed as she slipped behind a collapsed tree now exposed above the surface of the channel.

"You're not, um, going to go over the dam, are you, Esther?" Skitters asked with alarm as he hopped off her shell and onto dry land.

Esther put her nose up to Skitters' tiny face and replied, "I assure you I would never think of it."

Skitters shook with uncertainty.

"Hey! Listen to me! I promise, promise, promise you that is not why I came here," Esther mockingly assured the creature.

"I just don't want to lose you," a trembling Skitters told her.

"We, my little friend, are survivors. We were both given a second chance," Esther said to the water bug who was wiping his nose, sniffling. "Survivors who have been given a second chance do not surrender easily."

"But why risk going to the dam? Let's leave this place now." he begged.

"Because," Esther said slowly, "before the last drop of water trickles over the dam, I must resolve what happened to my mother."

Skitters stood silent, shuddering.

"She died trying to save me," Esther explained, "and I believe it is there at the dam my broken heart will heal."

"But, but. . . ." Skitters stuttered.

"I will return," Esther said as she winked at the tiny creature.

With that Esther departed. She paddled back into the increasing current of the channel and left Skitters sobbing on the bank.

As Esther paddled out rejoining the pull of the current, she heard an alarming cawing sound nearby. She raised her head upward scanning the treetops and spotted its familiar origin. It was Gack again, perched high above on a tree limb cawing his disapproval concerning her journey.

Esther stopped paddling, closed her eyes, and allowed the current to slowly pull her forward.

She began to flashback to her childhood recalling the very first time she had heard the alarming sound of Gack's caw.

In an instant she was dreaming again.

In her mind's eye Esther was three weeks old once more.

"Swim to the channel's bank!" Esther heard her panicked mother cry.

The alarming caw of the red-winged blackbird echoed overhead as the bird anxiously paced a tree limb.

The thunderous roar of the water rushing over the dam overwhelmed all other sound as Esther's mother swam with fury to reach her.

But rescue was futile. Esther's mother was unable to maneuver her child from the clutches of the dam and had now become caught in the current's overwhelming grip as well.

Esther's mother was rapidly swept away by the tow.

Baby Esther noticed a great blue heron step out from the shadow of a tree beside the dam. The enormous creature was observing her mother's plight.

The danger of the whole affair shook Esther as she watched her mother helplessly close in on the menacing metal structure.

Esther looked back to the blue heron and observed it teetering nervously at the channel's bank, putting a foot into the water only to draw it back ashore.

"Why doesn't that creature do something?" Esther whimpered.

The caw sound returned and it grew louder. Esther looked up to see the red-winged blackbird flying down to her at an alarming rate of speed.

Caw! Caw! Caw!

At that moment Esther shuddered and opened her eyes.

The flashback was over.

The dream had ended.

Today had returned.

She looked up at Gack presently perched high above in a tree cawing as he did on that very day so long ago. Esther resolved, *It will not happen again!*

The current gripped Esther as soon as she paddled round a bend. At that moment the monstrous dam came into view. She began moving but not by her own accord. She back paddled to keep herself steady.

It was as if she was following a path journeying backward in time.

She surveyed the surroundings and nothing looked familiar. Things had changed since she was a baby. The vegetation had altered appearances. The only thing that looked the same in her memory was the dam itself. It was an approaching metal beast.

Esther gazed defiantly on it as it rapidly drew her in.

Suddenly a figure emerged from the shadow of a tree next to the dam on the bank.

It was Mr. Berig.

I bet that evil creature would be delighted to see me go over the dam! a bitter Esther imagined. Her furious back paddling was rendered hopeless as she closed in quickly.

Swim to the channel bank! In her memory she heard her mother shouting.

In a panic Esther made a choice to attempt to swim ashore, but it was too late.

The unforgiving dam had her in its grip.

An anxious Mr. Berig took a single step out into the water next to the dam, and he teetered back and forth watching.

The violent undertow sucked Esther beneath the surface of the water. She drew her head and legs inside of her shell to protect herself and began to tumble inside a spinning current which relentlessly slammed her against the great steel wall.

I must get out of here! Esther cried inside. She pushed her legs back out and struggling to swim beneath the twisting fury she tried to reach the shore.

But her attempt was futile.

In a panic she pushed off from the bottom, surfaced, and grabbed hold of the steel wall's waterfall crest.

Her tiny claws violently scraped and slid on the dam's wet metal surface unable to secure a grip.

The situation had become critical.

In terror, a breathless Esther glared hopelessly over at Mr. Berig. She observed the creature stepping in and out of the water anxiously as if reluctant to do so.

The flow unmercifully began to push Esther atop the edge of the wall.

Mr. Berig began to span out his enormous wings and released a scream in anguish.

Esther took a deep breath and closed her eyes in silent prayer.

Miraculously the roar ceased.

The water level of the channel had dropped below the surface of the dam's spillway.

The waters behind Esther swirled to an eerie calm as the last drops dripped over the great structure.

Esther, exhausted and stunned, let loose her grip and fell back into the waters of the channel.

She paddled listlessly to the shore and crawled up on the land.

Gouges and scrapes etched her beautiful shell.

She glanced back at the dam and felt emptiness.

On the other bank, next to the tree, a weeping Mr. Berig cowered.

Esther slowly climbed up the bank and crawling around the great structure made her way to the other side and down to the rocks below at the foot of the dam.

These were the rocks on which her mother had lost her life.

As Esther pulled herself onto the boulders, she surveyed the retreating waters around her.

She looked up at the dam and was overcome with grief.

This journey had resolved nothing.

She had only felt the fear her mother must have endured that day, but the experience revealed no answers to comfort Esther. There was no reason why this all happened so long ago or who or what was to blame.

Esther lay alone upon the rocks, weeping. She slipped into unconsciousness.

FORGIVENESS

Slowly Esther began to stir. As she opened her eyes and drew them into focus, she could not believe what she saw.

Before her on the boulders at the foot of the dam were Boris the otter, Sir Elgin, the blue racer snake, Bosco, the bullfrog, and Mr. Berig, the great blue heron.

Was she dreaming?

"Good afternoon, dear Esther," Gack the red-winged blackbird pleasantly announced from his perch in a tree on the drying channel's bank. "I trust you had pleasant dreams?"

There was hushed concern among the crowd.

"You, of course, recognize everyone around on this occasion," Gack continued as he surveyed the gathering from his vantage point.

Esther focused her yellow eyes on Bosco and Mr. Berig in

CHAPTER TEN

particular.

"The channel is all but dry and many of us, I am sure, will be parting on our separate ways to find a new home," Gack observed. "I think it would be for the good of us all if we all spoke what was on our minds."

Gack looked about and every head hung in total silence.

"I see," Gack exclaimed as he was flying down to join the discordant lot gathered on the rocks. "We all have secrets, do we not?"

Skitters, who went unnoticed sitting atop Esther's shell, was very curious over the suspension of hostilities between the parties.

"No one is talking?" Gack asked, and tapped his talons on the stone. "I think the fact that we are all here, at this spot, where Esther's mother met her end says a lot, don't you?"

Everyone began sneaking brief, uncomfortable glances at the others.

"Well, then, I shall speak before any you. I trust if I get anything wrong, I shall be corrected."

Gack then surveyed the faces of Esther, Boris, Bosco, Sir Elgin and Mr. Berig.

"Perhaps I should begin with myself for I have a secret," Gack announced, looking at Esther.

Skitters' tiny eyes couldn't have been wider.

"Esther, I have never told you this since it would be much to your disapproval, but I am a dear friend to both Bosco and Mr. Berig. It is a fact I have concealed from you for the benefit of our friendship."

Esther's mouth went agape, but she kept silent.

"I imagine you think of me as a traitor."

Esther hung her head.

"Did you know, dear Esther, that Bosco, the bullfrog, and your mother were very good friends?"

Esther looked at the bullfrog.

Bosco nodded in affirmation.

"This took place long before you were born. During those three short weeks you shared with your mother, you probably were not a witness to this or were simply too young to recall it now."

Esther tilted her head with curiosity and raised an eyebrow at Bosco.

"You see, Esther, Bosco thought you were rather rash and unruly as a child," Gack explained as Esther's eyes widened. "Bosco doesn't like you because he believes if it were not for your shenanigans, your mother, his dear friend, would still be alive."

The frog looked at Esther with sadness in his eyes.

"It is time, dear Bosco, to let this go," Gack solemnly said.

The bullfrog nodded his head with remorse.

Gack next fixed his eyes on Sir Elgin, the blue racer snake.

Sir Elgin bowed his head and rested his chin on the rocks.

"I thought you blamed him for the death of your mother." Gack pointed his beak at Sir Elgin.

Esther drew her head back inside of her shell as if ashamed.

"I mean, please, dear Esther, do make up your mind. If you prefer, there's always Mr. Berig to blame. He did nothing, you know."

The small gathering had become incredibly anxious and still.

"If I recall that day, it was Sir Elgin who spotted you, Esther, swimming where the old row boat lay submerged. It was your forbidden playground. Tsk, tsk, dear Esther. A no-no. Your mother disapproved of you playing in that boat because it rested so hazardously close to the current of the dam. She drew a line there which, being disobedient, you crossed. Am I correct?"

"I didn't kill my mother," Esther said defensively.

"No, but if you will be quiet, dear Esther, I will tell you what did."

Esther blinked her weary eyes nervously.

"You, Esther, were headed to the old rowboat when Sir Elgin spotted you. Fearful you may become caught in the current of the dam, he raced upstream to inform your mother who then came after you."

Turning to face Sir Elgin, Gack inquired, "Does this sound about right?"

Sir Elgin nodded affirmatively.

"Killing the messenger, dear Esther?"

Esther looked at Sir Elgin and her lower lip began to quiver.

"So it's Sir Elgin's fault. If he hadn't told your mother, she would still be alive, correct?"

The anxiety level among the lot increased a notch.

"Then there's Mr. Berig," Gack murmured, looking about

the gathering of faces. "The great blue heron."

Mr. Berig didn't look so great at this moment.

Esther snuck her head out from her shell inquisitively.

"Mr. Berig and I have been good friends for many years, and he is perhaps the most tormented by what happened that day."

Esther listened attentively but with reluctance.

"Ah, yes, Mr. Berig. A more noble bird I have never known," Gack announced, "and a greater ruin I have never seen."

Mr. Berig began to slightly sway anxiously from side to side.

"You see, Mr. Berig saw your mother nearing the dam as she was attempting to save you, Esther," the blackbird explained. "Decisions sometimes are made with reluctance. It was not arrogance that prevented the blue heron from jumping in front of the dam to try to rescue your mother. It was fear!"

Mr. Berig turned his great head away. He could not face the others.

"For a split second, Mr. Berig considered he may lose his own life, and he hesitated." Gack stared at Esther. "This great creature's courage went over that dam, too, dear Esther. Mr. Berig does not live a day without thinking of it."

Esther gasped as Mr. Berig turned his head in her direction and their eyes met.

The great blue heron hung his head with remorse.

"Boris here," Gack continued, looking at the otter, "recovered your mother's body from this side of the dam and gave her a proper burial."

Esther looked at the otter with surprise. Boris twitched his whiskers.

"It has been a secret Boris keeps, but unknown to him it was an event I witnessed that day."

Boris nervously began twitching his tail.

"Do you know why Boris doesn't speak to you, dear Esther? It is not because he doesn't like you. Boris avoids you so he will never feel obligated to reveal the sordid details of what he discovered that day. A friendship with you would have only led there."

The otter nodded his head and peered into Esther's eyes.

"Compassion by avoidance," Gack called it. "Strange, but it is practiced by many."

Esther's eyes suddenly widened, and she turned her head to whisper into Gack's ear.

"The turtle shell scale in Boris' hut?" Esther whispered.

"Now you know who it belonged to, Esther," Gack whispered back, "and why Boris regards it so highly."

Esther trembled, surveyed the company, and retreated back into the security of her shell.

Gack suddenly hopped atop Esther's back and began pecking on her shell.

"Hello? Is there anyone home?" he cackled.

The remark brought smirks among the gathering.

Then Esther slowly snuck her head back out from her shell.

Gack touched his beak to Esther's nose and whispered, "Do you know what killed your mother, dear Esther?"

Esther shook her head, and muttered a soft "No."

"It was love," Gack whispered. "It was her love for you."

A single tear rolled down Esther's painted cheek.

Then, glancing at all around him Gack spoke out loudly, "Love killed Esther's mother. Nothing else."

The creatures all slowly drew close to Esther and began to huddle around her. A great warmth brushed over them.

"Love!" Gack repeated loudly. "It seems to me there hasn't been too much of that around here since Esther's mother passed away."

Staring imposingly beneath crunched eyebrows, Gack whispered, "She would not be too pleased."

The last trickle of water then disappeared from the channel below the dam like vanishing tears of anguish.

Esther spoke softly.

"It was you, Gack, who swooped down, grabbed me by the tail, rescued me from the water's current, and dropped me safely onshore that day," Esther reflected. "Why did you do that?"

Everyone's eyes fixed upon Gack. The blackbird turned and stared at the tiny water bug sitting atop Esther's shell.

"Why? So you could save him, Esther."

Esther glanced back and Skitters smiled brightly.

"Life is about helping each other, Esther," Gack explained. "When we help someone, that gift is passed on to another."

The huddle drew closer to Esther like a blanket of benediction.

"You see, Esther, the day your mother died we all made choices that would affect and change our lives for better or for worse. This was never just about you, dear Esther. It was about all of us."

Gack touched his beak to Esther's nose again and whispered, "You survived the dam again. Quite courageous I would think."

Then Gack added, raising an eyebrow, "But please do understand, dear Esther, the greatest act of courage today was forgiveness."

Gack nuzzled Esther aside of her cheek and muttered into her ear. "Rest assured wherever you are headed next in life, I will find you."

Esther grinned and replied, "Oh, I'm sure you will."

Esther gazed upon the spectacular horizon with uncertainly and surrendered a sigh.

"The future is a big place, Gack," observed an anxious Esther.

"That is because it holds such enormous promise, dear

Esther," Gack replied.

Esther nodded in agreement.

"Let me leave you with one last thought," Gack said as he straightened up and flapped his wings ready to take to the sky.

"Love took your mother's life, Esther, but life without love is to have never lived at all."

Esther looked at Gack with her bright yellow eyes and her lower lip began to quiver. "Gack," she said, "I don't believe I have ever told you I love you."

Gack cackled gently and shook his feathered crown.

"Oh, yes you have," he whispered. "Your eyes say it each and every day."

The turtle glanced at the blackbird.

Gack winked at Esther and uttered but four final words.

"I love you, too!"

With a gracious leap, Gack took flight to the sky and disappeared high over the treetops.

The other creatures nudged Esther with compassion and slowly departed on their separate ways.

Skitters hopped up next to Esther's ear, and whispered, "Wherever you are headed, can I go with you?"

Esther gently turned her head back and addressed the tiny creature with a smile.

"I wouldn't think of going without you."

As Esther crawled from the rocks onto what was once the channel bank, she noticed some squiggly lines on a damp log resting there. She inquisitively began to examine them.

"What are you looking at?" Skitters inquired.

Esther didn't reply. She began crawling around the log following the whimsical scribbles. Soon a familiar image from her past came into view. She sniffed and then nudged the snoozing creature with the tip of her nose.

"Hey!" a tiny voice cried out, "You should watch where you are going."

The tiny creature turned around to see what had wakened him and Esther sported a bright smile.

"Hello, Doodles!"

"My word! It's Esther!" the surprised snail shouted. "I haven't seen you since you were a baby playing in the rowboat."

"I am all grown up now." she said with a sparkle in her eyes.

"That I see, sweet Esther." the awestruck snail declared, staring at the turtle.

"Last we talked Esther, I recall you imagined you would live in the channel all of your life," said Doodles, surveying the empty passage. "It doesn't appear that is possible now."

"I have plans," Esther said.

Skitters suddenly rapped Esther on her head.

"Ouch!" Esther responded, "I mean, we have plans."

Esther grimaced as Doodles and Skitters exchanged cordial smiles.

At that moment Esther heard a familiar gentle flutter of wings overhead. She looked up and observed her secret friend, Dee Dee the Monarch butterfly, graciously soaring high above her against a brilliant blue sky.

Esther suddenly felt uplifted as if she were in flight herself, and a warm, comforting sensation grew within her.

Images of Madame Sweeney, Jeeter, and Bull Beckett raced through her mind's eye.

Then Esther could feel her mother's warm tender embrace as if she had never departed.

"So you are off to find a new home I presume?" asked Doodles, commanding Esther's attention.

"A better home," Esther replied with confidence.

"Will your mother be journeying with you?" Doodles inquired.

"Yes!" Esther took a deep breath. "She will always be with me."

Doodles tilted his head, greatly curious about all of the time that had passed. He stared deeply into Esther's eyes. "So what has happened in your life since last we met?"

Esther grinned and slowly blinked her bright yellow eyes.

"That would be like following the squiggly path you leave backward, Doodles," replied Esther, "and who would wish to do that?"

"You do not wish to look back, Esther?" Doodles asked.

"No!" replied the turtle with a shake of her head. "For where you are headed is more important than where you have been."

With those familiar words Esther said goodbye to the snail. She left this place full of hope, courage, faith, and forgiveness.

Esther never looked back again.

THE
END

Another Great Book by Kevin Scott Collier

barthpenn@heaven.org
Kevin Scott Collier
ISBN: 0-9752880-2-4
Price: $10.95

Heaven has gone high-tech! An imaginative story about 10 year-old Jordon Mink who received an email intended for a deceased man late for his appointment in heaven. The sender was Bartholomew Pennington, the angel on duty when he was scheduled to arrive. This is actually a journal record of their eventual correspondence and friendship as lessons are learned and miracles performed.

Other Exciting Books from Baker Trittin Press

Books especially for Tweeners
and those who love them.

Big Rig Rustlers
ISBN: 0-9752880-1-6
Price: $10.95

Todd and Amanda are invited to spend spring break with their uncle, aunt, and cousin Drew on their Wyoming ranch. When a band of high-tech cattle rustlers are caught, Todd learns why stealing is wrong and decides to choose a new path for his life. He also learns not to judge people by the rumors he has heard about them.

Legend of the White Wolf
ISBN: 0-9752880-3-2
Price: $10.95

They didn't call him a liar, they just didn't believe him. Brian was determined to prove his story. His sensitivity when he rescues a wolf pup from a steel trap results in a mysterious relationship with surprising results. Frequent visits with a God-fearing Native American adds a sense of connection with the past and his unique culture.

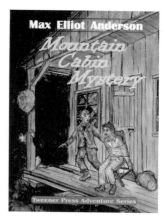

Mountain Cabin Mystery
ISBN: 0-9729256-3-5
Price: $10.95

Scott Holcomb and his friends had waited over two years for their wilderness camping adventure. Curiosity and a Kodak moment was enough to cause them to leave the trail. Surrounded by a dense fog and faced with a menacing bear, a remote cabin seemed to offer a temporary shelter, but. . . .

Newspaper Caper
ISBN: 0-9729256-4-3
Price: $9.95

Tom Stevens was a super salesman. He and his friends delivered newspapers early every morning. Along their route they often saw some strange things. Then one day they actually became the story. Their adventure is a reminder of the importance of friendship and that God isn't just for emergencies.

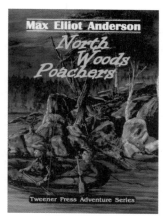

North Woods Poachers
ISBN: 0-9729256-8-6
Price: $10.95

The Washburn families have been going to the same lake, catching the same fish for about as long as Andy can remember. He is sick of it. This summer would be different he decided. In the end, Andy learns the concepts of family tradition and that God loves justice while He hates injustice.

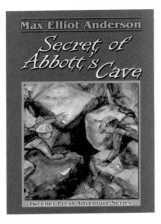

Secret of Abbott's Cave
ISBN: 0-9752880-0-8
Price: $10.95

Randy and his friends had a detective club and pooled their resources to buy a police radio scanner. After learning of a bank robbery, they went on a camping trip and cave exploring, discovered the hidden loot from the robbery, and questioned if they were really heroes. Who are the real heroes in life?

Terror at Wolf Lake
ISBN: 0-9729256-6-X
Price: $10.95

Eddy Thompson was known for one thing and one thing only. Eddy was a cheater. He cheated on anything, anytime, anywhere until something happened at Wolf Lake. It wasn't the brutal cold. It wasn't when he fell through the ice. It wasn't even when two scary men arrive at their remote cabin. What happened would change Eddy's life . . . forever.

BAKER TRITTIN PRESS

Order Information

If your favorite bookstore does not have Tweener Press titles in stock, you can order them directly from the publisher.

Call 888-741-4386to order today!

or

Complete and mail the form below.

PLEASE PRINT

Name_____

Address_____

City _____State _____Zip_____

Phone_____ email _____

Method of payment: Check___ Money Order___ Visa___ MC___

Credit Card # _____ Exp _____

Three digit number next to signature on back of card _____

Name on Card _____

Signture_____

Mail order blank with check or money order payable to:
Baker Trittin Press, P.O. Box 277, Winona Lake, IN 46590

Qty	Book Title	Price	Total

$3.50 for shipping and handling for one to four books. If five or more copies are ordered, free shipping and handling.

Merchandise total	
Shipping & Handling	
Subtotal	
6% Indiana Sales Tax	
Total Due	

Indiana residents add 6% sales tax

Tel: 888.741.4386 or FAX 574.269.6100